BLOOD FROM A STONE

A DI FRANK MILLER NOVEL

JOHN CARSON

DI FRANK MILLER SERIES

MAX DOYLE SERIES

Final Steps
Code Red
The October Project

SCOTT MARSHALL SERIES

Old Habits

BLOOD FROM A STONE

For the G Man.
The best friend a man could ever hope for.

ONE

Detective Inspector Frank Miller walked into the cool of the pub and saw his friend sitting alone, nursing a pint.

Detective Sergeant Andy Watt looked up when he saw his friend and colleague approaching. He waved over to the barman to get another pint.

When Miller had his drink, he sat opposite Watt.

'What's so urgent, Andy?'

Watt looked around to see if anybody was listening, but the small crowd that was in was interested in anything else but their conversation.

'Thanks for coming at short notice, Frank.'

'I could tell there was something wrong.'

'Really? Who says you aren't a good detective?'

'I don't know; who *does* say that?' Miller sipped at the cold lager.

'Figure of speech, son,' Watt was in his fifties, more than twenty years his boss's senior. 'But how did you know it was trouble? Maybe I enjoy your company so much that spending eight hours with you isn't enough.'

'First of all, you live all the way up Colinton, so I'm guessing you didn't go home and then come all the way back down here. I'm guessing you stayed late at the station again then came here to meet me for a pint, because there's something wrong in Wattville.'

Watt took a drink. 'Very astute. Here, take a look at this.' He reached into the inside of his jacket pocket and took out an envelope, which he passed over to Miller.

Just then, one of the city pathologists, Kate Murphy, came in. She saw the men and smiled. 'Hello boys,' she said, coming over to their table. 'Mind if a lady joins you? I'm buying.'

'Not at all,' Miller said, keeping the envelope out of sight.

'I won't argue with that,' Watt said. 'A couple of pints would be great.'

'Coming right up.' She went up to the bar.

'Not another one,' Miller said, waving the envelope about.

'Fucking twice this week.'

Miller took the letter out of the envelope and read it.

2

· · ·

Hi Andy! Things are getting wrapped up here. I do hope you're as excited as I am! I can't wait to see you again. I've never told this to a man before, but you took a hold of my heart that night and kept it for yourself. That's why I know that cupid struck us both.

As for the other things, well, it's getting sorted. I'm not going to tell you all the plans now, cheeky! I have a few surprises up my sleeve for you. But you will be delighted! We are going to get together soon and I will tell you all about myself. All the things I didn't get a chance to tell you that night.

'Jesus, Andy.'

'Don't act too surprised. I did tell you that I had slept with her down in Langholm. I told you when we were still there, if you remember.'

'I know. I wasn't too surprised, but this is a shocker. Did you promise half of the family fortune?'

'I know I'm a good-looking charmer—'

'And modest with it.'

'—but I think I must have done a real number on her. Without meaning to. But read on.'

· · ·

3

I want to be with you so much, Andy. You are my whole world now. Nothing else matters but you. When we are married, we will find our own little place, just the two of us. I want that more than anything. I will see you soon my love.

All my love from your wife,

Eve

'Fuck me.'

'Don't say that too loud in front of her if you ever meet her again. But look at the wording; *When we are married.* God Almighty. She's in love with me, wants us to get married and she's signing it, *your wife.*'

Miller tucked the letter back into the envelope as the barman was serving Kate.

'I mean, it's not as if I've been leading her on. It's been three months since I've seen her.'

'How long before you received the first letter from her?' Miller asked.

'A week.'

'A week? Christ, Andy, you should have nipped it in the bud, mate.'

'I did try; I ignored her. I thought she would forget about me.'

'Apparently not. And she knew you were in a rela-tionship?'

Watt finished the last of his lager, waiting for the fresh pint to be brought across. 'Not exactly.'

'What did you tell her?'

'Not a lie. I told her I was divorced.'

'Oh God.'

'You don't think she'll come up here, do you?'

'I do actually.'

'How can you be so sure, Frank?'

'The last letter you showed me a week ago. And bearing in mind I haven't read the other letter you got this week, but the last time, the postmark was from Langholm. This one is postmarked Edinburgh. Unless she got somebody to come up here and put it in a mail box for her, I'd say she is up here already.'

'Oh fuck.'

Kate brought two pints over and her G&T.

'Cheers boys.'

'Cheers.' They clinked glasses.

'What's been happening? I haven't seen you in ages,' Kate said.

Andy slept with a doctor down there, lied about his relationship status and now she's here in Edinburgh, stalking him. Miller held the words at bay. 'Not much after the to-do in Langholm,' he said.

'I heard the story from Percy Purcell. That must have been a nightmare.'

'It was rough. But everybody is fine.'

They stayed a while, talking shop.

Neither man mentioned Dr Eve Ross.

TWO

Miller woke up the next morning with a headache, not because of the drink but because Andy Watt was the first thing on his mind. Or rather, a woman who was already marching down the aisle with him, in her own mind. He couldn't believe the shit Watt had got himself into.

'What do you think?' Kim asked him as he poured some coffee.

'Hmm? Oh, nice.'

'It's my first day back at work and that's all you can say? *Hmm*. This is the third outfit I've tried on. I bet you never even noticed the first two.'

'I have a lot on my mind.'

'What did Andy want last night?' She struggled to keep her balance as she put a pair of high heels on, then kicked them off again. The flat shoes it was.

'Oh, he's having problems with Jean. He just wanted to let off some steam.'

Miller held out a mug for her but she shook her head. 'I've just put my lippy on.'

'At this rate, you're going to burn yourself out. You'll be falling asleep at *Coronation Street* again.'

Kim laughed and kissed him on the cheek. 'Nonsense. I've been getting myself in shape for weeks now. I want to make an impression on the boss on my first day back at work.'

'Your mother's the boss. The whole Procurator Fiscal's office is waiting to welcome you back with open arms. You won't have to make too much of an impression.' He took a paper napkin and wiped his cheek where he thought the outline of a pair of red lips were.

'Down a bit,' she instructed, watching him trying to get the lipstick off. 'Over a bit to the left. No, my left.'

She took the napkin from him and wiped his face. 'Now I'll have to do my lippie again.'

'Don't forget to take your curlers out.'

'Yeah, in thirty years time, that's the sight you'll be waking up to. It's coming for you, boy. Don't fight it.'

'With the amount of hair I have left, I won't have to worry about curlers.' He drank some of his coffee. 'When's Elaine due?'

Elaine was the new nanny who Neil McGovern, Kim's father, had vetted. He was in charge of a witness protection department for the government, heading up the Scottish office. The girl had come back clean.

The doorbell rang. 'Right now,' Kim said.

'Hi, Frank,' Elaine said, coming into the kitchen.

'Hi Elaine. Ready for the madness?'

'Ready, willing and able.'

'This is Kim's first day back as you know, so she might be running about like a headless chicken,' he said to her.

'I prepared myself last week. I appreciated Kim wanting me to shadow her for a whole week, and two days this week before going it alone. But I have ten years' experience. I'll be fine.'

'Glad to hear it. Kim's been on edge about going back to work.'

'I'm just about to get Annie and Emma's breakfast ready, so if you'll excuse me.' The young woman bustled away into the kitchen where Emma was playing with Charlie, their cat. Annie was stirring in her cot in her own room.

'It's such a beautiful day,' Kim said, coming into the kitchen for coffee.

'It is June,' Miller said. 'Even Edinburgh has one day of summer every year.'

'Looks like today is it.'

'It doesn't seem like it was only three months ago since you got cut off in that town because of all the snow.'

'It hasn't put me off going skiing if that's what you're worried about,' Kim said.

Just thinking about Langholm sent a shiver down his spine. What had Andy Watt been thinking when he'd slept with the doctor?

―――――――

DS Andy Watt groaned as his alarm went off. Jean wasn't in bed next to him. He was in the spare room. Then he remembered; they were having *issues*. He'd heard Jean talking on the phone to her sister.

What issues? He liked a drink, certainly. He was good to her on his meagre salary. Jean was minted but didn't flaunt her wealth. They lived in her huge house in Spylaw Park. They had been living quite happily until *she* turned up.

Then they started having *issues*.

The *she* in question was Jean's daughter, Abi. After Jean's divorce, the daughter had left for London at sixteen to live with her father and hadn't spoken to her mother in ten years. Now the bad penny had rolled back into town after Jean's ex had died.

Watt rubbed his eyes and sat up. Now he was in a room without its own en-suite bathroom, something he'd gotten used to.

The daughter had been given the run of the other wing of the house. Which sounded much grander than it was. It was a big house, and the wing was an extension that Jean's second husband had wanted built before he died.

He got up, grabbed his towel, and went for a shower.

The sun was streaming in through the bathroom window. The light hit his eyes and made him groan. Christ, why did he have to drink so much last night?

Kate Murphy.

That was the reason he was so hungover. He remembered Miller had gone home, then he and Kate had sat and chatted for a little while. Then he had walked her home. She was such a good laugh. She had invited him up for a beer. *No coffee,* she had said, laughing.

Then he had got a cab home and had got into the house as quietly as possible, but still, the daughter had been watching out of the window, watching him getting out of the taxi and, if not exactly staggering, gently weaving side to side as he walked up to the front door.

After that, things were a blur. He hadn't seen Jean,

and she was already gone for work when he got downstairs.

The house was empty. Or so he'd first thought. Abi was in the kitchen in this part of the house, despite the other wing basically being self-sufficient. It had two bedrooms, its own bathroom, living room, and kitchen, but ding dong, the witch wasn't dead, she was alive and well and standing in his kitchen, choreying his coffee.

'Run out of Sunny D?' he said.

She spun round. 'What?' she sneered at him.

'That's what all the kids drink, isn't it?'

'Piss off.'

'Toilet mouth. Does your mother know you talk like that before you kiss her goodnight?' Watt walked over to the toaster and took a packet of bread out of a cupboard. Popped in two slices and put the packet back before taking a packet of painkillers out of another cupboard.

'You think you're so smart, don't you?'

'I do actually, and thanks for asking.' He took the painkillers and washed them down with a glass of water. 'Don't you have supplies in your own part of the house? Or don't you like paying for your own stuff?'

'I could ask the same of you,' she said, turning her back on him again and pouring water from the kettle into the mug of instant. He stepped up after she got the milk from the fridge. She poured and put the carton back, making him get it for himself.

Watt knew that he could never like this young woman. If either of his own daughters treated him this way, he would have been raging, but they never had, because he had brought them up better than that.

'Just exactly what is it you want?' he asked her. 'I mean, your mother wasn't good enough to stay with ten years ago, apparently.'

'I just want to make up for lost time,' she replied. 'Not that it's got anything to do with you.'

'I live here too.'

She laughed at him, but there was no humour there. 'We're alike then; sponging off my mother. Except there's one big difference; I'm flesh and blood, and you're some washed-up old sod who can't get it up.'

'You'd be an expert on that, wouldn't you? Having old men get it up for you. Pay well does it?'

'Go fuck yourself.'

'I can't get it up, remember?'

Abi took her coffee and started storming out of the kitchen before she stopped and turned to face him again. 'You'd do well not to fuck with me.'

'Again... your opinion of me warrants that impossible.'

'Don't say you weren't warned.'

As she left, Watt knew that he and Jean would need to sit down and have a chat.

THREE

Angel walks the earth.

That was the thought doctor Eve Ross had when she was sitting outside the house on Spylaw Bank Road. It was early morning, the sun already up and rush hour in full swing, although it was quiet in this upscale residential street.

'Aren't you going to go and knock on his door?' Angel asked.

'What do you think?'

'Hey, there's no need to be snarky. I'm here for you, remember?' Angel, a young woman who only Eve could see, sat beside her in the front of the car. She had been Eve's constant companion for the last three months, ever since she had reappeared down in Langholm. After Eve had stopped taking her meds.

Her friend and confidant, Professor Simon Larking, was proud of her, he had told her. He had insisted she keep taking the meds. Eve had other ideas. Now she had moved on, and she didn't need the drugs. She needed Angel, who was right here with her. Angel had been with her ever since *that time*. Many years ago. When Angel had been the light when all she'd been able to see was the shadow looming over her.

'*Are you crying?*' Angel said.

'No.' The hot tears were running down her face. 'Yes.' She turned to Angel. 'What if he doesn't want to see me?'

'*Of course he does.*'

'Then why is he still with *her*?' They sat and watched the Jaguar come out of the driveway after the electric, wooden gates opened. The blonde woman was in the driver's seat.

'*You have to give it time, Evie. Those things don't happen overnight.*'

'It's been three months. He didn't write back, didn't call me. It took me forever to find him. Anybody would think he doesn't want to see me.'

Then Eve looked in the rear-view mirror. Saw the shadow sitting in the back of the car and she gasped. Looked round, her face contorting.

'*You're not going back to that place, Evie. I won't let you. You're just stressed. Let me deal with things.*'

Eve looked back at Angel beside her and reached

for a paper hanky from the packet that sat between the seats. 'Okay. It hasn't worked so far, so we'll do it your way.'

Angel grinned but there wasn't any humour in her eyes. Just pure hatred. *'You relax, my beautiful Evie. Relax and let Angel take care of things.'*

They watched the wooden gates close.

Andy Watt was nowhere to be seen.

Not yet.

FOUR

'This is not going to go down well with the people who live across the road,' Miller said as they got out of the car.

The office building was on the periphery of the New Town, only now it was earmarked for demolition and developers were fighting over it.

Miller came out of the back door to the loading bay. It had a brown steel fence around it. Emergency vehicles were parked along from the loading bay area, but the gate had been opened for the mortuary van.

Gibb drew on the cigarette again. 'Give me the rundown before I go in.'

'This building belonged to the Scottish National Bank and the staff moved out to Gogarburn. They've decided to sell it off, but being part of the New Town, or New Town North as it's being hailed, they won't just sell it to anybody. The company who buys it must have a plan in place so it can be accepted by the council. Some interested parties have already had designs drawn up.'

'We're dealing with a bunch of yahoos, then?' Watt said.

'If you mean people with money, then yes.'

'I suppose this old pile will go for a fortune,' Gibb said, sucking the life out of his cigarette.

'It will,' Miller said. 'Take a look at the top of this street; there are two tenements joined together. They're staying. But there were small buildings over there, belonging to a bakery before they were pulled down.'

They all looked across at an open site with a waist-high fence round it.

'Over to the right at the back of this office block is an open site with a huge one-level garage block.'

They looked over to where the previous access lane was now blocked off with concrete barriers and a swing-arm gate.

'The new project will encapsulate all that old car park and the garage area, this little bit of land here and the whole of the office block will be torn down. It will be built right round those two tenements,' Miller said.

DS Steffi Walker walked down the short street

towards them, holding two coffee cups. She handed one to Gibb.

'Thanks,' Gibb said. Although the sun was out and it was warm, he drank the hot coffee like his life depended on it. 'I was up late working,' he said to Steffi.

'Yeah, that's what it was,' Watt said.

'I want to make myself look a bit more presentable before Purcell gets here.'

'He's already here,' Miller said. 'He's upstairs with Maggie Parks and Kate Murphy.' He looked at his two male colleagues.

'Where's our coffee?' Watt asked Steffi.

'Still in the coffee pot in the wee café round the corner.'

'Forget S Walker from now on. You'll be known as R Slicker.'

'Better than R Soul.'

'That's no way to talk about DCI Gibb.'

'I was talking about you, as you well know.' Steffi made a face at him.

'How can you possibly come out with that?' Watt looked at Gibb. 'That's what we get for promoting her to sergeant.'

'Just wait until she's an inspector. She'll have your ging-gangs in a vice.'

'His what?' Steffi said.

'Ghoulies,' Miller answered.

'Oh yeah. Ghoulies in a vice. I like that.'

'Stop encouraging her, for God's sake,' Watt complained.

'Right, gang, let's get up there and see what our esteemed leader is wanting us to do.' Gibb had Steffi hold his coffee while he straightened his tie and then took the cup back before heading indoors.

Up on the fourth floor was a buzz of activity.

'Don't touch anything,' Maggie Parks ordered everybody when they trooped into the large, open-plan office space.

'I bet she didn't tell Paddy that last night,' Watt whispered to Miller.

Gibb heard and threw him a look. 'From what you told us, that's what you've been hearing for the last two weeks.'

'That's not very nice, really, eh?'

Detective Superintendent Percy Purcell waved them over. 'Christ, you look rougher than a badger's ar...' He saw Maggie watching him. 'Armpit.'

'I was up late working,' Gibb said, feeling his face go red.

'Working on what?'

'Her,' Watt said under his breath.

'Stuff. Things around the house. A bit of DIY.'

'Whatever it was, it certainly wasn't do it yourself,' Watt said to Miller.

'Smarten yourself up before you come to work, Gibb,' Purcell said. 'This isn't Professional Standards. We do real work here.'

'I'm sure Harry McNeil would appreciate that sentiment.'

'I don't care what he thinks. This is the real world we're working in and we have a real stiff here.'

Gibb looked at Watt. 'One word, and I will kill you on the spot.'

'Scruffy, hungover, *and* insane. Got the whole package going this morning.'

One of the other pathologists, Jake Dagger, walked into the large room, which Miller assumed looked much larger now it was devoid of desks and other furnishings.

'Ladies and gentlemen, please excuse my tardiness. I was at the locale of another incident.'

'You were in your pit,' Watt said.

'A very fortuitous guess, had it been correct.' Dagger grinned at him.

'Somebody else's pit. I hope she doesn't charge by the hour.'

'Much to your chagrin, I'm sure, but this particular lady had been in the docks for some time. Her features were, as you might say, rank.'

'I thought that's how you liked them, Dagger?'

'Alas, I like them to have a pulse, Andy.' He walked over to stand beside Kate Murphy, who was looking down at the star attraction.

A man dressed in what had probably been a stain-free suit when he left the house, was now sitting in a chair with his hands tied behind his back. The suit was now in need of a good cleaning as it was soaked in blood. A spear was sticking out of his chest.

Purcell was standing close by, observing. 'I'm assuming the uniforms have started the door-to-door?' he asked Gibb.

Gibb flicked a look at Miller who imperceptibly nodded.

'Yes, they're out there now.'

'Good. I want all the stops pulled out on this one.'

'Who's the victim?' Miller asked.

'Rick Dempsey,' another voice answered behind them. A woman. Everybody turned to look at Procurator Fiscal Norma Banks walking into the room, her voice echoing off the walls. Miller looked behind her and saw his wife coming in. She wasn't Kim Miller, detective's wife at that moment, but Kim Miller, PF Investigator. She gave him a brief smile, and just for a split-second, he wondered where his girls were.

'Rick Dempsey,' Purcell reiterated. 'I called the PF when we got an ID, and if you shower hadn't been skiving outside drinking coffee, you would have known that by now.'

'How did he depart this world?' Kim asked as they approached the body.

Kate Murphy looked at her. 'He was opened up in the front and the spear rammed in, but his head's at an awkward angle. His neck could be broken.' Dempsey's shirt had been pulled closed but not buttoned up after the forensic officer had taken photos. She opened up his shirt again.

He had been slit from his navel to his throat. Organs were spilling out, held in check by the shirt.

'Jesus, that would give anybody the boak,' Watt said.

'A sharp knife did this. Not a serrated edge, but a very sharp smooth edge,' Kate carried on.

'The spear?' Purcell said.

Kate shook her head. 'No, that's there for show. That weapon couldn't have been used. It's too awkward and unwieldy.'

'Who was this Dempsey?' Gibb said, the colour leaving his face.

'He was an architect,' Norma said. 'We haven't contacted next of kin yet, or his office, but his face has been in *The Caledonian* recently. He does some work for George Stone.'

Miller looked at his mother-in-law, still not

believing that she was now related to him through marriage. 'Stone? Less surprising that he's dead then.'

'Why?' she said, and it was almost like everybody in the room turned to him to hear his speech for the defence.

'You know him as well as I do. Nothing ever sticks when it comes to George Stone. Anything illegal that the wind blows in his direction is deflected.'

'Agreed. Make sure Dempsey's next of kin are informed then go talk to Stone. I can only pray to God that we can get something on him.'

'That would be nice,' Watt said, 'but I wouldn't put money on it.'

'Try. Without crossing the line of course, sergeant. Kim will be liaising with you, and she'll be back with MIT as of this morning.'

'Welcome back, Kim,' Purcell said.

'Thank you. It's nice to be back.'

'And when you're sick of looking at his ugly mush, we can have lunch sometime,' Watt said.

'I'll take you up on that.'

'I'm right here,' Miller said.

'Oh, I don't think you have anything to worry about, Frank,' Norma said, giving Watt a look. 'I'm going back to the office now, but I want a daily report.' She walked out of the room alone.

'What was she trying to say?' Watt said.

'What sort of time did he depart this life for a better one?' Purcell asked.

Kate looked at her watch. 'Nine forty-seven now, so we're talking seven to eight hours. One, two o'clock this morning.'

'Isn't there security in here?' Watt asked.

'There's one guy,' Miller said.

'Where was he in relation to this floor?' Gibb said.

'That's what we're trying to ascertain now. But from what we can gather, everything is locked up and he just checks the perimeter.'

'There's nothing in here but copper pipes,' Purcell said. 'All the good stuff was taken out. But if the guard wasn't on the ball, then somebody could have gotten inside.' He looked at Maggie Parks. 'Have your crew found the entry point yet?'

Gibb looked at Watt, waiting for the wisecrack. Watt just shrugged and held his hands palm up.

'Apart from the large car park at the rear, there's a small management car park right at the back of the building. One that meant they could just stagger from their cars up a flight of stairs and inside. It was that door that was opened. Not forced, but opened.'

'I can see from all the blood that he was murdered here, tied to that chair,' Purcell said. 'But what are the symbols drawn on the walls?'

They looked to the wall where some little symbols had been drawn in blood.

'I have absolutely no idea,' Maggie said.

'Get plenty of photos and we'll get them to a cryptologist. Meantime, we'll get onto looking for any CCTV images that might have captured them coming in. I want to know if Dempsey here came in willingly or if he was brought here for some reason. And whether he came here alone and was followed, and why they killed him here.' He looked at Miller. 'Make sure you have another word with that guard. I want a full background done on him.'

'Yes, sir.'

Miller started walking away. 'Andy, come with me and we'll talk to the guard now.'

FIVE

Abi Melrose hated Edinburgh with a passion. Hated her mother too, when push came to shove. Leaving this hole to go and live in London with her father had been the best decision she ever made.

Jean was okay, but a lot stricter than her father had been. He had let her smoke pot and drink and go out with boys and stay out overnight. She had had so much fun with him. Of course she'd had boyfriends, but none that she ever felt like she could spend the rest of her life with.

She still felt an ache inside when she thought of her father. The thought of coming back home to live with this old boot had made her sick, but the alternative was to take up a position as a whore at King's Cross.

The first thing Jean had said to her when she

stepped into the house was, *I hope you don't smoke.* She had told her that she didn't, but the truth was, Abi smoked, drank, and fucked with the best of them. She would just disguise it, and if she got caught smoking, then she would say that she didn't want Jean to be disappointed in her. But she didn't think she'd have anything to worry about. Jean was all about having her wee girl back, and Abi had to admit, this was a comfortable house.

Now all she had to do was figure out how to get rid of the sponging old bastard who had moved in like a heat-seeking missile.

And she thought she had just the thing. It was the smell that grabbed her attention. She had met the postie at the door and took the mail from him. There was nothing for her, she was just being nosy.

Mostly bills and junk mail but one stuck out because it smelled of perfume. She read the name on the front; addressed to Romeo of course. From some woman called Eve Ross, with an address in Langholm, wherever the hell that was. Strange though, because the postmark was from Edinburgh.

Hadn't her mother mentioned that the old sod had been down in Langholm, working on a case, back when the bad snow storm had struck? The name rang a bell but she hadn't given it much attention. Until now.

She put the mail down on the kitchen table but put

the letter on the counter to keep it separate from the rest.

Then she decided to have a look in the bedroom. Abi knew her mother and the old cop were having problems, but it was over her, not some letters he had been getting. She wanted to know if this was the first one, but she suspected it wasn't.

Although Watt was staying in a spare room – he'd had three to choose from in this wing of the house – he had taken the one furthest away from the shared bedroom.

She went into the bedroom they used to share. Jean had made the bed. It was a habit that Abi hadn't inherited from her mother. She'd taken her cue from her father and left her bed unmade until it was time to go back in it.

But her mother was a neat freak. There wasn't a speck of dust anywhere. If it was up to her, she'd have a cleaning woman come in and do all the hard work, but she had promised her mother that she would keep her side of the house clean. Which she hadn't.

She started pulling out drawers, having a look at where everything was before moving it. Nothing. Then again, none of his clothes were in here. He'd emptied his wardrobe and drawers and moved it all into the other room. Abi could see the light at the end of the tunnel and the day when the old bastard moved out. They had taken an instant dislike to each other.

She went along to his bedroom. He was like her, leaving his bed unmade. There were clothes strewn about on a chair. Stuff littered every surface. She opened his drawers, which were surprisingly tidy compared with the rest of the room, and started going through them, not bothering to memorise where anything was. If he found out she'd been in here, then fuck him, she would just say she had been snooping and so what? One day she would fall heir to this place, and he would be long gone before that happened.

Nothing in the drawers. It was hot in this room, which faced south. He probably never cracked open a window. It smelled of beer and stale farts. She walked over to the wardrobe and opened it. What in God's name did her mother see in this man? He wore cheap clothes, nothing like the expensive stuff her mother wore. Granted, her father wore cheap clothes, but he *chose* to. He would never give his hard-earned to the capitalist scum who had their goods made in sweat-shops by children who worked for next to nothing.

There were a couple of shoe boxes up on a shelf. She pulled the first one down. Just cheap knick-knacks. Photos and the like, of two young women.

The next one held what she sought; more letters.

She took them downstairs to read.

SIX

'They had one fucking job. Pair of clowns.' Adrian Jackson walked back and forth in his office in *The Pinnacle*, a hotel he had bought on Edinburgh's George Street. He had been out of the American prison he had been in for twenty-five years, for about six months, but was slipping back into the Edinburgh lifestyle very nicely.

He looked over at his nephew, Brian, to see the young man playing a video game on his phone.

'Are you listening to me?'

'Aw, Aide, I'm almost done.'

Jackson walked over, his walking cane by his side and smacked his nephew's phone out of his hand.

'Fuck me, that hurt,' Brian said, pulling his hand back.

'It'll hurt even more when I shove this up your arse.'

'I hope you don't talk like that to Fiona.'

'It's fucking Aunt Fiona, and if you call me Aide one more time, I swear to God...'

'Sorry, alright? I just like to play a couple of games in the morning to get my mental juices flowing.'

'You play that thing because you're a lazy bastard.' He stomped back to his desk and swivelled in his chair. 'Did you even hear what I said?'

'About me being a lazy bastard? Yes, I did, and if you think that didn't hurt, coming from my favourite uncle—'

'I'm your only uncle, baw bag.'

The door opened and Rita Mellon walked in with two coffees. 'I can hear you both from out there.' She looked at Brian. 'Get the door, that's a love.'

'It's that pair of twats that my nephew there said would be good for the job at hand.'

She handed him a coffee and sipped at her own.

'Where's mine?' Brian said.

'Brian, love, I can only carry two coffees, one in each hand, so where do you think the other one is?'

'In the coffee machine?'

'You're such a smart boy.'

Brian got up, picked up his phone and was about to walk out. 'I'll just go and make one now.'

'No you won't. Sit on your arse. We have a problem and you're in the middle of it.'

Brian pulled a face like he was smelling something that was stuck on his shoe before sitting back down.

'Put the bloody phone away or I'll chuck it out the window. Rita, make yourself at home.'

'Thanks, Adrian. Is Fiona coming? I haven't seen her in here for a wee while.'

'No. I don't want her hanging about here any more than she needs to. She's managing the bars now, keeping an eye on things. Keeping herself busy.'

Rita sat down. 'What's the problem we're having?'

'You know an old mucker of mine said he knew some good guys if we wanted to go ahead and set up the security business?'

'Of course.'

'Well, dip wad there said he knew a couple of blokes who would be perfect for the New Town North job. All they had to do was turn up, keep an eye on the place and report back directly to me. Nobody would look at them twice. I gave them a van, uniforms, paid them well, and one of the useless arseholes was sleeping in the van at night. Sleeping, I tell you.'

'That doesn't bode well for him.'

'It most certainly does not. But one of them, Creepy baws—'

'Crawley,' Brian said, interrupting.

'Baws. He had the foresight to send me a text before Norma Banks came in with one of her staff and issued warrants on the spot so they could look through the phones. He told me they were being interviewed and then they have to go to the station to make a formal statement. Then they're meeting us at a neutral location.'

'Why are the police talking to them?'

'Didn't you hear the news?'

'No, we were busy this morning.'

'Please don't enlighten me. I know you're divorced from Mad Malky Mellon now, but I ask you to never reveal the sordid details of your relationship with my nephew.'

'It's all thanks to you paying somebody to get Malky to sign the papers that I'm finally free of him. He doesn't know we're living in the swanky new flat in Quartermile.'

'I wish you had kept the wee Porsche that came with the flat,' Brian said.

'It was ostentatious,' Rita said.

'I thought it was red. Why you bought a Mini I'll never know.'

'Anyway, getting back to the problem here before I forget what the fuck I'm talking about,' Jackson said, 'we have to try and deflect anything that comes near us regarding Rick Dempsey. The man who was murdered in the office block this morning.'

'Wasn't he the architect you hired to draw up plans for the new site?' Brian said.

'No, dimwit. He worked for George Stone. If your head wasn't full of wee men on that game thing, maybe you'd know what we're talking about. Dempsey and his team at the office have drawn up a cracking plan, but it seems that somebody is not happy with us stepping on their toes. I want to talk to those two clowns after they've been to the cop shop.'

Rita shook her head. 'Nobody says that anymore, Adrian. *Cop shop*. Don't say that outside.'

'In this day and age, I think people have more to worry about. Right now, the one thing we have to worry about is lying in a fridge in the city mortuary.'

SEVEN

Miller found the guard around the corner in an office. He was sitting on a chair with two empty chairs opposite him. No other furniture was to be found.

'Why would they leave some chairs behind?' Watt said to him as they entered the room.

Davy Dickson looked at him, his eyes bloodshot. 'Surplus to requirements. The whole lot will get chucked out apparently.'

'Right, Davy, let's go over this again,' Miller said. Watt took out a notebook as they settled down opposite the security guard.

'As I told the others, I was sitting in my van. I'm not paid to be in the building, just to do security checks on the perimeter.'

'You have keys though, right?' Miller said.

'In case I see something going on inside.'

'Did you have any reason to use them through the night last night?'

'No. I got out every hour and walked round the perimeter. There was nothing unusual.'

'You physically checked the locks?'

'Every one of them. Including the front. They were locked at all times.'

'Which way was your van facing?' Watt asked. 'When you were sitting in it?'

'It was facing the loading bay doors. At the side of the building.'

'And that would still give you good visibility if somebody came up on your left-hand side and went into the little management car park.'

'Of course.'

Both detectives looked at each other before Miller spoke again. 'How long do you think we've been doing this job?'

'What?'

'Let me answer for you; a long time. We've sat opposite killers, rapists, men who touch kiddies. The worst of the worst. And you know what? Every single one of them lied to us. We get used to it, can spot the signs a mile off. So when you sit here and tell us you sat in your van, alert and keeping your eyes open, I know you're lying. Just by looking at your body language.'

Dickson fidgeted for a moment. 'Are you trying to

say I wasn't here last night?' He raised his voice, confirming Miller's suspicion.

'No, I'm not saying you weren't here. But you certainly weren't paying attention. Somebody got in through the side door from the management car park and you didn't see them come in. So what were you doing?'

'I resent this kind of questioning.' Dickson sat back with his arms folded.

'Too bad,' Watt said. 'Have you seen the corpse through there?'

'No. Des, the dayshift guy came on and he brought coffee and we sat and gabbed for a wee while. Then he came in for a quick walk around, just to make sure everything was okay, before he had to sit outside. I came in for a pish before I went home and while I was in the toilet, Des found the body and started shouting like a wee lassie.'

'So tell us what you were doing during the night when somebody brought the victim in and murdered him?' Watt said. 'Or maybe I should say, how many cans did you have?'

'Are you suggesting I was drinking?'

'That's exactly what he's suggesting,' Miller said. 'You look not just tired, but like you've been drinking and then fell asleep.'

Dickson hung his head for a moment before sitting

up straight again. 'Look, it gets boring sitting on your arse in a van all night, only getting out for a quick squint at the doors. Nobody ever comes round here at night. So I had a couple of tinnies.'

'Nobody comes round here at night, except for last night when a psycho walked in and—'

Dickson held up his hand before Miller could finish. 'I know, you told me; somebody killed somebody. Gives me the fucking heebie-jeebies that. I mean, what if he had come out and thought he hadn't had enough for one night and decided to pop me as well? '

'Tell us about your co-worker, Des Crawley,' Watt said.

'Creepy? He's a good guy. We've worked together since day one. He's sound as a pound.'

'You think he could have come round in the middle of the night while you were having a wee sesh to yourself?'

'Of course not.'

'Do you think you would have noticed your colleague coming round to the building?' Miller said.

'Obviously.'

'Whoever came in used a key. They unlocked the door and let themselves in.'

'That van doesn't have air conditioning, so it gets hot at night, and I might have had one tinny too many last night. I fell asleep until this morning when Creepy came round to my window and knocked on it like he'd been sniffing glue. How anybody is so cheery in the morning is beyond me. There should be a law against it.'

'And that was the first time you'd seen him since coming on duty... at what time?'

'Nine last night. We do twelve hours on, twelve off. Then some other blokes take over at the weekend.'

'It's possible then that Crawley could have come round when you were drunk and got in without you seeing him in the middle of the night?' Watt said.

'It's possible. I had my first tinny at midnight. Had a wee read of my book. Ate my sandwiches, washed them down with another lager, then I did a patrol, came back, had another lager then I got in the back of the van and had a kip.'

'You told us you checked every hour,' Watt said.

'Then you caught me in a lie. I obviously didn't literally mean, every hour. I meant every hour*ish*.'

'Bit uncomfortable in the back of a Ford Transit isn't it?' Miller said.

'I have three cushions from an old settee, and a blanket in case it gets cold, so I get my head down and have a good night's sleep. This night shift is doing my napper in. I thought it would be an easy number, which it is really, but it's this walking around once an hour that gets boring. So I get my head down.'

'A pipe band could have come down to the back door and you wouldn't have heard them, would you?'

'Not really,' Dickson admitted. 'I never thought for one minute this sort of thing would happen. It's just a ratty old building that they're going to pull down. Who cares?'

'Somebody did,' Watt said.

'We'll need you to come back to the station and make a formal statement,' Miller said. 'Then we'll have a wee chat with your colleague.'

They left the room and by the time they got back to the open room, Rick Dempsey was in a black body bag waiting to be taken down to the loading bay.

'What do you think?' Purcell asked Miller.

'The guy was sleeping in his van all night. Somebody could have brought Shergar in here and he wouldn't have noticed, but I'll have his background checked out.'

'Let's get Dempsey's background checked out as well. Somebody wanted him dead and I want to know why.'

EIGHT

'I think I'll walk. Brian, Rita, you two can come with me,' Adrian Jackson said. 'Have a couple of the boys come as well. We can have a stroll along Princes Street since this is the one day of the summer when it's not pishing down.'

'Where we going, Adrian?' Brian asked, grabbing his suit jacket from the coat stand in the corner of Jackson's office.

Jackson stood looking at his nephew. He'd only been reconnected with the boy since he came back to Scotland but still the boy didn't know to call him Uncle Adrian. *Only Adrian in front of other people, fucking wank muffin* he had told him, but it hadn't sunk in yet. Maybe if he jabbed him with a cattle prod every time he slipped up, Brian would get the message before sunset that day.

Brian was in his late twenties, and his girlfriend was in her early forties, and although the two of them went together like sugar and vinegar, it was working for them. Now that Jackson had let them live in one of the apartments he had acquired a few months earlier.

'We are going to see a friend of mine. None other than Robert Molloy.'

'Do you want me to call ahead and see if he's available?' Rita said.

'Rita, you do look after me so well as my personal assistant, but I took the liberty of procuring a tête-à-tête with Mr Molloy myself. He's expecting me for afternoon tea, or perhaps a cool gin.'

'Tea and crumpet with Molloy? You're getting very close to him. Maybe he's got a thing for you,' Brian said.

'That's right, mock away. And while I'm in Molloy's office having a nice cool drink, I'll tell him of your concerns that maybe he's turned homosexual. In this day and age, it's acceptable. In fact, some of my best employees are homosexual. They're great people, Brian. You know, normal human beings. But since I know Robert Molloy, and he was brought up in a different age, he might take exception to you saying that he and I are in a relationship. And we all know what he's like when he gets upset; people find themselves being detached from a favourite body part, or in the case of females, having something inserted into them. And coming from Robert Molloy, that's not as exciting as it sounds.'

'Jeez, cool the jets there, Unc.'

'Brian, let me start to make something straight; my name is Uncle Adrian. In front of other people, you may call me Adrian. If you call me *Unc* again, I'll thrash the living daylights out of you with my walking cane.'

'Threats now? Deary me, Adrian. You know I'm your favourite nephew. I don't think for one second that you would lift your cane to me.'

Jackson whacked the cane over Brian's backside, making the young man jump. 'Next time it's over your fucking tadger.'

'Fuck sake. Maybe you should have taken up wood-working in prison instead of some obscure, Chinese form of self-defence.'

Jackson pulled on a lightweight summer blazer and they left the hotel. The two bodyguards were waiting at the front door, and after a walk along George Street and down onto Princes Street, they were at Robert Molloy's new hotel on the North Bridge.

'I'm sweating like a mule,' Brian complained when they got inside the air-conditioned building.

'That's appropriate, 'cause you're a fucking donkey. Now stop whining and go and sit in the bar with the boys. Mrs Mellon and I will be going upstairs.'

'I bet you say that to all the girls,' Rita said.

'I do actually. Mind Brian doesn't get jealous.'

'I can hear you,' Brian said.

'You were meant to.' Jackson turned to one of the guards. 'Stan, make sure Brian only has a couple. If he gets out of line, you have my permission to throw him out of a window into Waverley station. Make sure Benny is keeping his eyes peeled too.'

Stan smiled. 'Yes, sir.'

'He was talking hypothetically,' Brian said, not wanting to turn his back on the big man.

Jackson and Rita were shown upstairs. Robert Molloy's desk was over by a window but they were shown over to a settee on the other side of the large room.

'This used to be a bedroom but I thought it suited my purpose far better,' Robert explained, pouring some drinks.

'It has its own toilet,' Michael Molloy said, coming in. 'Now his bladder is old, he can go for a pish without leaving the room. Although I think he used to do that anyway.'

'Shut up. We have a lady present.'

'Mrs Mellon. Good to see you again. You lost weight?'

'I have, Michael, thank you for noticing.' She smiled at him.

'If I wasn't in a relationship, I would ask you to dinner. I hear you too are being swept off your feet these days.'

'I am indeed.'

'And not by that ape you were married to.'

'No. For some reason, he signed the divorce papers all of a sudden.'

A look was exchanged between the three men.

'Good. All's well that ends well, and all that. But please sit down.'

Jackson surmised that Michael wasn't being his usual obnoxious self because Rita was in the room, otherwise every second word would have been *fuck* or the conversation would have turned to how Michael was going to have somebody's nob removed with a chainsaw. He suspected Michael also had a soft spot for Rita, but his girlfriend might have a problem with him fooling around on her.

'I heard your house is finally finished,' Jackson said, sitting down on the settee with Rita. He couldn't care less about Michael's house but wanted to make small talk that didn't involve Rita's waist size or the colour of hair dye she used.

'It is indeed. I was having the old house refurbished but after it got burnt down , I hired an architect to design the new one.'

The Molloys sat down on chairs, and Robert put

coasters down on the coffee table in front of them. 'Don't want people to think we're riff raff,' he said. 'And that's what prompted Adrian's visit here today,' he continued.

A slight change came over Michael's face. 'There are two other major parties interested in New Town North; George Stone and Kerry Hamilton. Well, if I think that either of those fuckers topped Dempsey to scare us off, then the only concrete blocks they'll be licking are the ones round their ankles.'

Oh, here we go Jackson thought. It hadn't taken long before Michael's tongue started getting colourful. 'I'm thinking that they're the only two who had anything to gain, and we all know what Stone is like.'

'He's an arrogant fanny,' Robert said, 'nothing but a jumped-up brickie.' He looked at Rita. 'Do you know how that twat got started?'

Rita shook her head and picked up her glass.

'In the army. A squaddie, who couldn't shoot a water pistol by all accounts, and he served his time as a brickie. Came out of the army, started a contracting business and then a few years later, took over a large building company and then another until he was buying up every building company he could get his hands on. Some say by nefarious means. Now he's a millionaire. Un-fucking-real.'

'I assume we're going to pay him a visit?' Jackson said.

'You presume correctly. Along at that club he practically lives in. Pretentious wanker. I'll get some of the boys to come with us.'

'How do you know he'll be there?' Jackson said.

'I told him we're coming for a visit and it would be in his best interests to be there and meet with us. He doesn't want to fuck us around.'

'Sounds good.'

'Nothing personal, Rita, but this is a job just for us. You'd be better off staying at home.'

'I think I've just been insulted,' she said, with a smirk.

'No, you haven't. I just wouldn't want anybody to ruin your good looks,' Michael said. 'There might be some blood shed tonight, and it's not going to be ours.'

'I'd like for some of my men to come along tonight. The security boys. They're all ex-special forces. They could crawl up to that fucker's bed and he wouldn't know they'd been there.'

'That's a good idea. Let's get some planning done,' Robert said. 'By the way, I'm opening up my own private gentleman's club downstairs. It's going to be the most exclusive club in Edinburgh. Unlike that poofy place in Princes Street. And if anybody's a member there, get an invite out to them. In fact, I have the invites already printed. We could hand them out tonight. We'll soon have that place emptied. They'll have the best of gear here. You, Adrian, are an automatic member. Mrs Mellon too.'

'That's very good of you, Robert. May I suggest inviting the consortium as well?'

'I'll have to make sure they don't score too high on my riff-raff-ometer," said Robert. 'Most of them will be okay. But George Stone can bog off. He's a member along the road. He's not going to be a member here.'

'Let's get things sorted then,' Michael said, and Jackson could see a subtle change in the man, a dangerous version of him hiding just under the surface.

This was going to be fun.

NINE

George Stone's office was in Moray Place in the New Town. Like the other offices in the street, it had once been a home.

Purcell and Miller went into the reception room where a young woman sat behind a desk. It reminded Miller of the time they had been in this very street talking to some lawyers about a case.

'We're here to see Mr Stone,' Purcell said.

'He's not here.'

'I called ahead and was assured he *was* here.'

'He was. He's not now.'

'Where is he then?' Miller said, starting to get pissed off at the woman's attitude.

'He got called out to one of his sites. He's very hands-on.'

'Where is he?' Purcell said.

'Up at Craiglockart. There's a big project going on there. Mr Stone bought the old college campus and we're building townhouses and converting the old buildings into luxury apartments.'

'Call him. Tell him we're heading out there to speak to him. If he makes a habit of avoiding us, I'll have a team search for him and we'll make sure the media know he's helping us with our enquiries.'

'I'll pass the message on but he won't be happy.'

'Is this the face of somebody who cares?' Purcell said, and they walked back out into the warm afternoon.

'He won't be happy, indeed,' Purcell said as Miller got behind the wheel. 'And try to stay on the left-hand side of the road. Paddy told me how you nearly killed him on the way down to Langholm.'

'That was a little bit of exaggeration right there. I brought the car to a controlled stop under extreme circumstances.' He started the engine and drove off.

'Pish. Paddy said he nearly shat himself.'

'He's an old woman. Andy Watt never complained.'

'Andy Watt's got a screw loose. He probably had visions that he was on the dodgems or something.'

'I took the advanced driving course, remember?'

'That means bollocks to me.'

Miller headed south, hitting Lothian Road,

heading for Morningside. 'How's your dad getting on as an investigator?'

Purcell looked at him. 'I wish he would just age gracefully. Running about with Bruce Hagan like the two of them belong in a TV show. Luckily, Hagan doesn't have him climbing drainpipes or anything.'

'That you know of.'

'For God's sake, Miller, I'm nervous enough about my old man being out all night without you adding to it.'

'Hey, it's nothing to be ashamed of. I worry about Jack. He still does some jobs for Neil McGovern and although he tells me it's quite safe, I still worry.'

They got to Craighouse fifteen minutes later, in one piece. It was on the periphery of Morningside. Billboards flanked the main entrance and a little lodge house was at a side gate, with a sign telling them it was the marketing centre for the new development.

'I got in the wrong game,' Purcell said. 'I should have joined the army and trained as a brickie.'

'I'm sure not all of the squaddies went on to become millionaires,' Miller replied.

'What made him stand out though? Sure, he was a contractor, but to take over larger building companies. How did he do that?'

'He was in on the scam that was called the new

Scottish Parliament building. Just like all the other hounds who took our tax money.'

'This is true.' They approached a barrier, manned by a worker in a hi-vis vest and hard hat.

'Can I help you?' he said when Miller rolled down the window.

'Police. We're here to speak to George Stone. Do you know where we can find him?'

'Up in the main building. It's called *New Craig*. He was going there.' He lifted the barrier and they drove up the main road, looking at a mixture of apartments and townhouses on the right. Miller drove round to what was once the original building, parking next to a silver Range Rover.

The building was huge, and what Miller thought was probably Victorian, but to him, anything that looked this old was called Victorian.

Inside, they could hear the noise of people banging away. There was a box with hard hats sitting outside, so they took one each and walked inside.

They heard a voice booming round the great hall. 'Make it happen! I don't pay you to fuck around with this. My clients are not some white-collar workers, they're the elite. Make an effort man!'

George Stone turned to the detectives and was about to yell at them when Purcell held up his warrant card.

'We're here to speak to you,' he said.

Stone looked at them as if he was about to argue, then he smiled. 'What do you think?' he said, sweeping his arm about. 'The great hall.' They looked at the oak panelling and the classical pilasters.

George Stone was a big man, around six foot three and weighed what Miller guessed to be around eighteen stone, with a full head of black hair. He got the feeling that Stone himself was larger than life as he strode across to them.

'This place is beautiful, isn't it?'

'It's grand.'

'Come on, gentlemen, let's talk outside. I would give you a tour but there's a lot of construction going on in here.'

They went back out into the sunshine and both detectives put their hard hats back in the box.

'Do you know what this place was?' Stone said.

'No, but I have the feeling you're going to enlighten us,' Purcell said.

'It was an asylum! Can you believe that? This beautiful place housed the insane. Some people say that there are too many roaming the streets but they can't come back here. This is for the rich insane of Edinburgh.'

'We're investigating the murder of Rick Dempsey,' Miller said, before the big man got too distracted.

Stone looked puzzled. 'I'm sorry, I don't know the man.'

'I think you do, Mr Stone. He was an architect.'

'Oh, that wee cu... man. Nasty piece of work. Had a mouth on him. Oh, I'm not denying he had talent, and he did some design work for me, and with a few beers down his neck, he was fine, but when he switched to the whisky, he'd fight anybody in the bar. Even me, but I warned him well what would happen if he punched me.' Stone looked between the two detectives. 'That wasn't a confession. Dempsey never challenged me. When was he murdered?'

'In the middle of the night. The wee hours of this morning.'

'I was at home. In bed with the missus. She'll back that up. And my security team. I have twenty-four-hour security. Whoever topped Dempsey, it wasn't me.'

'I didn't think for one minute that a man like you would dirty his own hands, Mr Stone,' Miller said.

'That's very true. However, I had no beef with the man. His work was great, but he had a split personality.'

'With him out of the way, that would be one less plan to be submitted for consideration, in the sale of the bank building,' Purcell said. 'Maybe somebody trying to get rid of the competition?'

'All the plans are finished, superintendent. It doesn't matter if Dempsey's dead or not.'

'Unless there are changes to be made.'

'Dempsey is part of a team.'

'You know of anybody who would want him dead?'

'If you're looking for a suspect, then look no further than Kerry Hamilton.'

'The shopping heiress?' Purcell said.

'The very one. She just bought the old department store at the West End.'

'And why would she be interested in Rick Dempsey?' Miller said.

'I don't know that she would be, but she was interested in New Town North.' His mobile phone rang. 'If you'll excuse me, I have to take this. But have a word with Kerry Hamilton. And take an Alsatian with you.' He answered the phone and turned away.

TEN

'I thought since you're off for the summer that maybe we could do something fun,' Jeni Bridge said to her daughter, Lynn.

'I'm not twelve, Mum.'

'I know, I just thought—'

'I'll be seeing more of Mark over the summer.'

'Who's Mark?'

They were standing in the kitchen, Jeni waiting for the kettle to go off but now her instinct was to open the fridge and take out a bottle of wine.

Lynn rolled her eyes. 'I've told you about him many times. You never listen. Mark, as in my friend, Mark.'

'You never told me about this Mark.' The kettle clicked off and Jeni poured herself a coffee. Lynn was drinking a beer straight from the bottle.

'It's not *this Mark*. It's just Mark.'

'Does this Mark have a last name?'

'Denholm. And I've already told you about him.'

'When did you tell me about him?' She went to the fridge for the milk, saw the wine and almost wavered but didn't.

'For God's sake, Jeni. I told you about him weeks ago. I wish you would listen once in a while.'

Jeni poured the milk before putting the jug away, trying her best not to throw it across the kitchen. 'You know something? Ever since you went through to Glasgow for a visit and decided to stay, you've completely changed.'

'Oh, here we go. Here's the *where did my little girl go* lecture. Dad treats me like a grown up. Sharon does too. And besides, I stayed to help with the new baby. My new little brother, remember?'

'Yes, of course. I'm sorry. I've just missed you, that's all.'

'I know you have, but let me live my life a little. I'm going to uni after the summer break and I won't be seeing you for a while.'

'I'm not going to lecture you on campus life, I promise.'

'No need; I'm moving in with Mark.'

Jeni looked at her. 'You're what? Does your dad know about this?'

'Of course he does. Mark's a family friend of Sharon's.'

'Good God. What else has been going on?'

'Nothing. For God's sake, Jeni, I'm a grown up.'

'It's *mum* to you. When did you start to think it was okay to call me by my name? I'm your parent, not a friend.'

'Sharon thinks it's okay.'

'Sharon isn't your mother! I am!'

'Start acting like it.' She stood looking at her mother defiantly. 'I'm going out. I'll be staying over at Mark's for a while.'

'You're what? You only got here a couple of days ago.'

'I've made friends through there. I only came back to get my stuff.' Lynn turned and walked out of the kitchen. Jeni could hear her upstairs, opening and closing drawers.

The last piece of the jigsaw puzzle that was her life just imploded.

Jeni tried to keep her temper in check when her daughter came back downstairs. The thin tendril of her relationship with her only child was so fragile that she felt a strong breeze would break it.

'When will I see you again?'

'I'll call you. Maybe we could have coffee in town sometime.'

'I want you to write down Mark's address.'

'It's not his place. It's a friend's. She stays there and there's room for all of us.'

'Christ, it's not a commune, I hope?' And there it was; the tendril snapped.

'As I said, I'll call you.' And with that, Lynn closed a chapter in her life with her mother.

She grabbed her holdall and left.

Outside, sitting in a car with the windows rolled down, was Mark. He'd parked round the corner so Lynn's mother wouldn't see him.

Lynn got in and slammed the door shut.

'Is that door shut right?' Mark said.

'Yes.'

'I was being facetious. You nearly took it off the hinges.'

'Sorry.'

'It didn't go well with your mother, I assume?'

She shook her head.

He started the engine and drove slowly out of the estate onto Craig's Road. He headed down towards the bypass.

'Your mother knows you're with me though, right? That you'll be safe?'

'Of course. I told her that but she still pisses her pants.'

'Ach, you know what mothers are like. She'll

worry. You're her only bairn so of course she's going to worry.' He looked at her. 'She's used to dealing with stress in her job. You said she's a banking executive?'

'That's right.'

'And your old man too?'

'Yes.' She'd told her mother that Mark was a family friend of her stepmother, Sharon, but that was a lie. Her father had never met Mark, and Lynn was sure he wouldn't have liked him if he had.

'I'm a woman. I'm eighteen now. I know how to look after myself.' She opened the holdall that was sitting on her lap and took out a packet of cigarettes and lit one.

'Is that you hiding your fags in your bag?' Mark said, grinning.

'No.' She looked at him like he'd just suggested she was five and had pinched a lollipop from the corner shop.

'Relax. You're with me now and we're going to have fun.'

'Where are you staying? You do have a place, don't you?'

'Of course I do. It belongs to a friend of mine. She said we can crash there for as long as we like.'

'She?'

'Oh, don't get all jealous on me now. I have plenty

of female friends and I've never slept with any of them. They're just mates.'

'As long as she knows you're my boyfriend.'

He laughed as they got onto the bypass. 'Relax. We don't have far to go. My friend understands.'

A few minutes later they were taking the slip road for Sighthill.

They drove through the lights onto Gillespie Road, then left onto Pentland Avenue.

'Jesus. This is a nice part of town but look at that road,' Lynn said. The side street had massive potholes and looked broken up. Not in keeping with the neighbourhood at all.

'It's to stop people using them as a rat run my friend said. She warned me about this.'

At the top of the road, he turned right, and there it was, the double gate in front of the driveway.

It opened as if by magic, but it was due to somebody watching on the camera that was pointed down at them. A double garage faced them, but the driveway continued round to the left. Another, single detached garage faced them.

The side of the big house here is a separate wing. An in-laws' suite, my friend told me. It's where she stays.'

Just then, a young woman walked into view, smiling when she saw Mark.

'Hello, you,' Abi Melrose said.

Mark got out of the car. Hugged her. 'Is that old cop around? What's his name again?'

'Andy Watt, and no, he's not around.'

'Good.' He let Abi go and turned to the car and waved for Lynn to get out.

She got out and Mark introduced her. 'Lynn, this is my friend.'

Lynn shook her hand. 'Nice place you have here.'

'It's my mother's. I live in this part of the house. We won't be bothered by anybody. Or anything.' She giggled and walked away, holding Mark's hand.

ELEVEN

Bruce Hagan and his wife, Amanda Cameron, stood in their living room in the flat above Tanners Bar in Juniper Green.

'Jesus, you don't have to stand when I come into the room,' Adrian Jackson said. 'I'm not your commanding officer.' He chuckled as he entered and sat down. His bodyguards were downstairs in the bar, waiting for his two guests to show up so they could show them up here.

'You're the new owner, Mr Jackson. Just showing respect,' Hagan said.

'Listen, son, I know you were a copper, and we have a two-way street going here; I ask you to respect my privacy and use your wee flat when I want to conduct some business away from prying eyes. I don't charge you rent like the other tight wad who owned this place before me, and Amanda here got a healthy pay rise. I look after my workers, and that way we have a good working relationship. All I ask is you don't talk about me being here.'

'I know they looked after Bruce eventually, giving him a pension,' Amanda said, 'but he was put through the mill and nobody wanted to know when he was banged up in the asylum. Trust me, we won't be discussing any business with people outside of this room. And I did tell you that Bruce's ex is also a detective. I don't want anything to come back and bite us.'

'You did, and I appreciate that. You look after my bar, I'll look after you.'

She smiled. 'Thank you.'

They left the room, Jackson patting Hagan on the arm. He knew the man had been tortured and lost some fingers and part of an ear while on duty, then he had been doped full of experimental drugs which had sent him doolally and he'd ended up in a psychiatric hospital. Fast forward and he'd been released after they discovered he shouldn't have been there in the first place. And after more treatment as a day patient, he'd got his demons under control.

Now Bruce Hagan was a private investigator and his wife ran the pub.

There was a knock on the front door, the one that was at the stairway that led down into the pub. The door opened and Jackson's personal bodyguard – Roger Peck – entered. He was a big man with ginger hair, so his obvious nickname was *Ginge*. Only Jackson called him by this name.

'Sir, the two gentlemen to see you.' He ushered Des Crawley and Davy Dickson in.

'Thanks, Ginge.'

'Yeah, thanks, Ginge,' Dickson said, grinning.

Ginge gave the man a look that promised they would be having a little talk afterwards.

'Are you trying to have your tadger booted off?' Jackson said.

'What do you mean?'

'I mean sit down, both of you, while you're still in one piece.'

Crawley tried to sit on a big leather chair until Jackson whacked him with his walking cane across his knee. 'That's where I'm sitting, numb nuts.'

'Jesus, that fucking hurt.'

Jackson quickly pulled out the hidden sword from his specially made cane and pointed the tip at Crawley's face. 'Imagine how this would hurt then.'

Crawley gulped and sat down before Jackson got any closer.

'I think I just pished my pants a little,' he said in a whisper to Dickson.

Jackson put his sword away and sat down. 'Right, I

need you to tell me what went on last night. You, Dickson, start. And I don't want to hear any fucking drivel. Get to the point.'

'Right. I was feeling a cold was coming on, and I was worried that I was going to throw my ring all around the inside of the van, so I had a wee lie down, just five minutes mind, then before I knew it, Des here was waking me up. The cold medicine I took must have made me fall asleep.'

Crawley grinned and nodded, like the actor had remembered all his lines.

'Dearie me. You've had all day and that's the best pish you can come up with? Just because I was in prison, doesn't mean I'm a total arsehole. I didn't leave my brain back in America. Here's what's going to happen; you're going to tell me what really happened or else I'm going to have Ginge drive you somewhere quiet and lonely, with a shovel, and you'll be digging a big hole. Understand?'

'I told you not to make that shite up,' Crawley said.

'You're not any better, ya fucking maggot,' Jackson said. 'Why I don't have you both taken away and dealt with, I don't know. Well, I *do* know, but I'm saving that. If you tell me the truth, maybe we can salvage something from this.'

'I didn't think anybody would be round during the night so I had a few cans and got my head down,'

Dickson said. 'Just do what you're going to do to me. I shouldn't have done it, but I've always been a fucking moron. My mother said I'd never amount to anything and she was right.'

'God rest her soul,' Crawley added.

'Shut up,' Jackson said. 'At least he's got the balls to admit it. Which means he won't be detached from his. You, on the other hand, are about to get a vasectomy with my sword if you don't start telling me the truth. And you have thirty seconds. Go.' He looked at his wrist watch.

'Okay. Sometimes I leave early. There's nothing going on, and it's boring so sometimes I leave early and meet Davy for a pint.'

'Don't fucking rope me into this. When you meet me, I'm already off duty. You're the one who skives off.'

'Aw, fuck you—'

'Children!' Jackson shouted, and then the door opened and Ginge rushed in.

'It's okay, we're just having a discussion,' Jackson said. Ginge once again looked at Dickson, who didn't want to make eye contact, before he exited the room.

'You have a chance to redeem yourselves,' Jackson said. 'I have a job I need done. Yes or no?'

'How can we refuse?' Dickson said.

'Exactly.'

TWELVE

Lou Purcell stood in the middle of his son's living room, holding up a suit bag. 'Guess what this is and I'll buy you a beer.'

'Oh God. Do we have to? It isn't your old strait jacket, is it?' Percy said.

'Funny. Hurry up, for God's sake, my arm's getting tired.'

Suzy, Percy's wife came into the living room.

'Sit down, love and I'll get us a beer.' Percy went through to the kitchen and got them all bottles of beer.

'What's that you've got there, Lou?' Suzy asked.

'I already told Percy to guess.'

'You should just use a top hat for your magic act like the rest of them,' Percy said, coming back in with the beers and sitting down on the couch. He'd muted the TV but was still watching it.

'You still haven't guessed. You're slipping there, son. I thought you had a mind like a steel trap? Or a finely-tuned Swiss watch?'

'More like an old, leaky tap; it used to work fine, but over time, it became tired and weak,' Suzy said.

'For God's sake, don't encourage him. Before we know it, we'll have fallen asleep on the couch and he'll still be here, playing with his magic wand.'

'Will you just guess before my arm falls off?'

'Let me see; a dress jacket with tartan trousers.'

Lou lowered the bag even more. 'That wasn't a guess. That was cheating. Did Larry tell you?'

Suzy looked at her husband. 'Did you know what your dad had before he came here?'

'Look, in my own defence, Larry called me and asked me if you had picked up your costume yet.'

'It's not a bloody costume. Look.' He unzipped the bag and took out the jacket with the tartan trousers on a hanger. 'Pretty classy, eh?

'Why are you going as Rupert the bear?' Percy said.

'I think you'll look fine, Lou,' Suzy said, slapping her husband's arm. 'What's the occasion?'

'Me and Larry have been invited to a posh do. At the Holyrood Park Hotel in Prestonfield. Andy Watt's missus, Jean Melrose, is going. I saw the guest list.'

'Is it fancy dress?' Percy said.

'If it was, you could come along dressed as a clown, but nobody would know the difference. What do you think?'

'I think you'll look fantastic, Lou,' Suzy said.

'I think Rupert passed away and his family donated his trousers to Oxfam, and you just happened to be in there at the right time,' Percy said.

'Your attempt to make me feel bad is woefully lacking. You're only jealous because you didn't get invited.'

'Oh yeah, that's it. I haven't been invited to one of Andy Watt's piss-ups.'

'If you cleaned the wax out of your ears once in a while, you'd hear what I'm saying. It's his wife that's going to the party. I'm sure he'll be there, but it's not his do.'

'It's Watt's girlfriend, not his wife. And you do know that Robert Molloy just had a re-opening after he bought it and had it refurbished?'

'Of course I do. It was in *The Caledonian*.'

'I thought you just read the Beano?'

'It's more than you read. All your books start with *Once upon a time...*'

'How did you manage to snaff yourself a ticket to that? Or are you planning to gate-crash? More to the point though, have Sooty and Sweep been invited?'

'More beer?' Suzy asked.

'I think he's had enough.' Lou said, 'but I'll have his.'

'Hang fire there, old man,' Percy said, sitting more upright. 'I want to know more about this party before you start getting wired into my Becks. But mind you don't have too many or else you'll blow chunks all over your good Rupert costume.'

'And there's the green-eyed monster right there,' he said laughing as Suzy got up to go and get more beer.

'I am not jealous of some poofy shindig with a bunch of posh twats,' Percy said looking at his father, who was smiling at him.

'Mock if you must.'

'You know, if you smile like a weirdo like that at the do, you won't snag yourself any—'

Lou put his hand up. 'Before any filth comes out of your mouth, it's all respectable women who are going to be there.'

'I was going to say *sirloin*, but whatever. You still haven't told me how you got an invite.'

Suzy came back in with more beers. 'What did I miss?'

'Horny Harry there is hoping to go to the do and pick up some rich, ninety-year-old widow so he can let her have one look at his shrivelled old—'

'For God's sake, have a word with yourself,' Lou said.

'I was going to say, before I was rudely interrupted, shrivelled old pension book.'

Lou clinked bottles with Suzy and had a good chug out of the bottle. 'You need help. You're obsessed with talking about nobs.'

'You're the only one who's used that word tonight,' Percy said, laughing.

Lou turned away from his son. 'We got an invite because Larry's daughter is a friend of this Melrose woman. Jean Melrose is an interior designer, and she runs a few wee shops, selling vintage clothing for women.' He turned to Percy. 'I can give her your size if you like since you like trying on Suzy's clothes when she's out.'

'Bugger off. Suzy's a lot smaller than I am.'

'I've heard of Jean Melrose, come to think of it,' Suzy said. 'She's a high-flyer. I wonder how the hell she became interested in Andy Watt?'

'It takes all sorts,' Lou said.

'That explains why the daughter got invited, but how did a couple of coffin dodgers manage to get an invite?' Percy said.

'I swear to God.' Lou shook his head. 'I'm surprised you even made it through high school.'

'It's not my fault that you sent me to a dump of a high school. I should have been sent to a private school.'

'Pish. But we got invited because Larry's daughter asked if we could come along.'

'Nope.'

'Nope what? Are you just going to sit there and come out with random words?' Lou replied. 'They have special wards for people like you. You'll be happy there, after me and Suzy have you committed.'

'I meant, nope, I don't buy that for a second.'

'Jesus, there *is* a detective in there waiting to get out. But you're right. Me and Larry are going along to do some snooping for Bruce.'

'Your partner-in-crime, private investigator Bruce Hagan?'

'How many Bruce's do you think I know? Yes. He's the only one.'

'Snooping for what? How much silverware they have?'

'No. Larry's daughter, Linda, thinks that her husband is having it away with one of the other women who have been invited. She wants to do some snooping and eavesdropping.'

'Does she have proof, this Linda?'

'That's why we're going to be there. We've already followed the man, but he's being extra cautious. As far as Linda knows, the woman doesn't know her, but we're there as backup to see if we can hear anything.'

'That could be your new superhero names, you and Larry: Cloak and Dagger.'

'Isn't one of the pathologists called Dagger?' Suzy said.

'Yes, that blows it. They'll just have to be called—'

'Right, I'm off before there's any more slagging.'

'When's your party?' Suzy asked.

'Friday night.'

'Well, I think you'll look smashing, Lou.'

'Thanks, sweetheart.'

Lou walked down the hall with his suit bag, trying to ignore his son whistling the theme tune to Rupert the Bear.

THIRTEEN

Baby Annie was down for the night, Emma was in bed after a bedtime story, and Miller was sitting down with Kim. His father, Jack, was round with his girlfriend, Samantha Willis.

'I heard about Rick Dempsey,' Jack said.

'It's a bad one alright. They gutted him like a fish and left a spear in him.'

Kim nodded. 'I went down with my mother. It was a horrible sight.'

'Any motive yet?' Samantha said.

'Uh oh,' Jack said, 'Sam's on the sniff for ideas for her new book.'

Samantha Willis was an American crime writer, living in Scotland. She had moved in along the hall from Miller, and Jack had started dating her before moving in.

'Jack, I'm the sceptical one in the family.' She smiled at him and patted his leg. 'Besides, my new novel is set in America.'

'Who is this guy Dempsey?' Jack said.

'He was the senior architect for a firm that does a lot of work for George Stone, amongst others. Rice and Bailey.'

'They're a quality outfit.'

'I know. We're going to talk to them tomorrow. We had trouble tracking down Dempsey's next of kin. The media don't have a name yet, but now we've tracked down the wife, so the name will be released and we'll talk to the colleagues tomorrow.'

'Wasn't his wife suspicious when he didn't come home?' Jack asked.

'She said she thought he was staying out late with a client, which apparently happens more often than not. He's stayed out all night before. She left for work in the morning so she didn't think anything else about it. They're trying to get a hold of a daughter who's backpacking in Asia or somewhere.'

'Do you think Molloy is behind this? Or Adrian Jackson?'

'I don't what the motive is just now, but we're not ruling anything out. We spoke to George Stone today, but there's no way a man with his money would dirty his own hands like that. If anything, he'd have some people do it. But why kill the man who designs things for you?'

'Maybe he was annoyed that Rick Dempsey didn't draw up a better design than Molloy's designer,' Samantha said. 'I mean, maybe Stone saw it that way.'

'Molloy's design will be revealed at a party on Friday,' Kim said. 'At the Holyrood Park Hotel. I asked around and it seems that Molloy's design *is* the leading one.'

'That would certainly give Stone a motive for murder. Also, Kerry Hamilton. They're the only other two finalists.'

'We'll talk to George Stone again tomorrow,' Miller said. 'But tonight, we can just enjoy the peace and quiet. The bairns are sleeping so we try to appreciate the quiet times.'

'Listen, we'll get going,' Samantha said.

'Grandpa!' Emma shouted, running into the room. 'Grandma!'

Samantha laughed and gave the little girl a hug. 'I guess quiet time is over,' she said, laughing.

***

'That was quite the wee swally last night, Kate,' Andy Watt said as they got up from the table.

'For you, maybe. I just had a few and poured you into a taxi.'

'What? Naw. I had to hold you up all the way down the road, doc.'

'Andy, obviously working in MIT has rattled your brain a little bit. You, my darling, were, what do you call it? Blootered.'

'That sounds funny when you say it.'

She playfully slapped his arm as they were putting their jackets on. 'You coming down for a nightcap?'

'Nightcap? It's only nine o'clock woman.'

'Early nightcap.'

'As much as I'd love to...'

Kate held up a hand. 'Sorry. I forgot. The wife.'

'Girlfriend. About to become ex, by the way things are going.'

They went outside into the fading light. A chill wind ran down the High Street from the castle.

'You just touched on the fact you were having problems when you came home with me last night.'

'We were having a laugh, and I didn't want to bother you with the details.'

'It hasn't stopped you in the past, Andy Watt.' She smiled at him.

'How about you, Kate? How's your life doing?'

'My life or my love life?'

'Both. But get to the good parts. I have to get home.'

Although he doubted that Jean would even care what time he got home. 'Come on, I'll walk you down the road.'

'Wow, a gentleman. I need to mark this on the calendar.'

'Hey, that hurt. I have feelings you know. Underneath this ruggedly handsome exterior, I am a human being.'

They started walking down past the tourists, going past John Knox House, and the end of the world, as it once was, many moons ago.

Down St Mary's Street and then into Holyrood Road. Watt felt comfortable with Kate, probably more comfortable than he had felt with Jean for the longest time. Or ever? He didn't know. Kate was the real deal. She laughed with him, and she was honest, and on more than one occasion, she had cried in front of him. After one drink too many, and they had laughed about it afterwards. But she was good company, and that was something he was needing right now.

They got to her apartment block down near the Scottish Parliament building.

'Not too late to come up for a... what shall we call it... *evening cap*?'

'Well, since you are so persuasive, how can I turn you down?'

They went up to the apartment, with darkness falling down over the city.

'No boyfriend waiting to jump out with a baseball bat?' Watt said as they walked into her kitchen.

'No boyfriend waiting to jump out holding anything,' Kate said, taking two beers out of the fridge.

'Cheers,' he said. 'You got a bottle opener?'

'It's a screw top, genius.'

'I knew that. I was just curious whether you had a bottle opener for future use.'

'Next time I'll pour us a couple of shots.'

'That's my girl.'

They sat down, Watt on the couch and Kate in a chair. 'You deserve to have somebody in your life, Kate. You're too nice to be on your own.'

'You offering?' she said, smiling.

'I mean it. And this is me sober. I usually blether when I've had too much to drink, but I've only had a few tonight. But it's none of my business. I'm just a nosy old sod.'

'Hardly old, Andy.'

'I'm fifty. Anything north of forty is old, according to the youth of today.'

'I'm forty-two. So we're a pair of old codgers.'

'Here's to us old 'uns,' he said, and raised his bottle in salute.

'How come you're having such a bad time with Jean, if you don't mind me asking.'

'Her daughter left for London when she turned sixteen. Went to live with her old man, but now her old man is dead, so she's come running back to mummy.'

'And you don't like her?'

'I have this gut feeling, Kate. I just don't trust Abi at all.'

'It must be hard for a copper like you to just sit back when you have a feeling about somebody.'

He didn't know whether she meant Abi or herself and could feel his cheeks going red.

'Nobody special in your life, Kate?'

'How many times have you asked me that, Andy. Sometimes I get so lonely. I haven't been out with many guys after Jimmy.' Jimmy Gilmour, who had been a detective on Watt's team.

They chatted for a while, having another couple of beers and then Watt stood up to leave. 'You know where I am if you ever want to chat,' he said to her.

'We could do dinner one night if you like. I haven't been out for ages. Except for a girl's night out with Kim and Hazel Carter.'

'That would be great.'

She kissed him then, passionately. 'Let's make it a real date then,' she whispered.

Outside, a wind was running off Arthur's Seat.

Maybe it was the beer, but he had a strange feeling inside when he thought of Kate. And the kiss. He had no words.

He flagged a taxi.

The reception committee was waiting for him when he got home. Jean, her daughter Abi, and two people he didn't know, a young man and woman.

'What?' he said.

'We need to talk,' Jean said. Abi smirked and no introductions were made, although Watt thought he recognised the young woman but couldn't be sure.

'Uh oh, the big talk,' he said, his attitude fuelled by the alcohol.

He followed Jean upstairs into her bedroom, thinking that maybe he'd got it wrong. He hadn't.

'And just who the hell is Eve Ross?' She picked up the letters from her dresser and flapped them about like a fan.

'You've been snooping through my things while I was out? Classy.'

'No, Abi did. And just as well by the look of things.'

'Look, you were out and about doing God-knows-what, and I thought it was the beginning of the end.'

'That's a poor excuse,' Abi said from the doorway.

Watt turned round to look at her. 'I never trusted you from the minute I clapped eyes on you.'

'The feeling was mutual, but it looks like I was the one who was proved right.'

Watt turned back to Jean. 'It was nothing. It was meaningless.'

'You thought I was cheating on you, you bastard?'

'Something like that.'

'You're a disgusting pig.'

'Emphasis on the *pig*,' Abi said.

'Shut up,' Watt said to her without turning round.

'That's it. I've had enough of you,' Jean said. 'Pack your stuff in the morning and get out.'

He took a step towards her and snatched the letters out of her hand. 'You know one thing? At least Eve was fun. And I'll pack my stuff tonight.' He left the room, brushing past Abi and went along to his own room. He pulled the suitcase out from under the bed and packed his things. He reflected how sad it was that his life's possessions could fit into a suitcase and a medium one at that.

He went downstairs where they were all having a good chin wag. Mark got up from the table and approached Watt.

'Abi said you were getting a bit lippy with her, mate.'

'Is that right, fuck face? If you want to talk about it, then fine by me, but I've had dealings with a lot harder fuckers than you. And if you do happen to get the better of me, then I know a lot of bad bastards in this city. Not coppers either. So come ahead.'

The cogs were turning behind Mark's eyes, and he obviously thought better of it. He just sneered and sat back down.

'I'd appreciate it if you could forward my mail to the station,' he said, but Jean was sitting at the table crying.

'What? The letters from your fancy piece?' Abi said.

Watt turned and walked out, closing another chapter in his life.

FOURTEEN

'In the name of Christ,' Robert Molloy said as they stepped out of the taxi on Princes Street. 'How in the name of God is anybody supposed to get around in this city when they stop fucking cars going everywhere?'

'We could always have a wee chat with some of the councillors. They're all a bunch of fannies anyway,' Michael Molloy said.

'Get a grip of yourself. We won't be coming back to this shitty little club again, so don't worry about it.'

'You're the one who's moaning.'

Adrian Jackson stepped out of the taxi behind with Rita Mellon and Brian. A minibus was behind and six men got out. Behind that, another minibus. Six more men, associates of Jackson.

'We could have come in the minibus and saved on a taxi,' Michael said.

'What? Are you on drugs? It's bad enough sitting in a fast black where somebody no doubt spewed their fish supper all over the floor. Or pished on the seats. Fuck knows what they get up to in there. No wonder they have vinyl seats. Manky piece of shit. But it's still a step up from some poxy minibus that could have been used for God knows what. If they allowed vans, we could have used our own but we don't want to give the constabulary an excuse to stop and have a fucking neb at what we're doing.'

Michael gave the driver some money and Jackson came up to them. Michael smiled at Rita.

'You certainly scrub up well, Mrs Mellon.'

'Thank you, Michael. You're not so bad yourself.'

'Let's get in this dive, then we can have a drink somewhere.'

'I do hope you mean with my boyfriend, Brian?' She smiled at him.

'I meant all of us, dear Rita, as you well know.' He looked away from her at Brian, who was standing looking around him. Michael closed his eyes for a second and shook his head.

'Right, we going in, Robert?' Jackson said as his men stood behind him.

'Yes. I'm dying to see their faces when the working class walk in.'

One of the men walked up to the anonymous

brown door that was tucked in between two shops. No signs, nothing to suggest there was a gentlemen's club behind the door.

A few seconds later, a man dressed not dissimilarly from a butler, looked at the men like they were a bunch of football hooligans.

'Can I help you?' he said, making a face like he smelled something.

'Nope,' Michael said.

'We're here to see a friend of ours,' Robert said. 'We have an invite.'

'Oh, I don't think so. We don't invite parties in here.' He was about sixty, with a croaky voice, but he looked like he was ex-military and was used to going toe-to-toe with people in a bygone age.

'Just get the fucking door open, Grandpa,' Michael said.

'I beg your pardon?'

'You heard. Move. I'm freezing my fucking baw bag off here.' Then Michael seemed to remember that Rita was there. He turned to her. 'Please excuse the French.'

'Oh, the French use the same word for scrotum as we do? Interesting.'

Michael laughed as he barged into the club, followed by his men. The others followed.

The door was closed behind them. 'This is highly inappropriate,' the old man said.

'George Stone,' Robert Molloy said. 'Take us to him.'

'And what do you want here?' another man said, standing in front of them.

'Who are you?' Robert asked.

'My name is Colonel Sanquer. I'm the head concierge here.'

'Sanquer rhymes with wanker,' Michael said matter-of-factly.

The older man looked at him like he would have pointed a rifle at him many moons ago. A muscle twitched in his face. 'What do you want?'

'George Stone is expecting us. Take us to him. Now.' Robert was starting to get annoyed and was on the verge of having the old boy escorted somewhere.

The man started walking down an oak-panelled hallway and then turned left into a large room. George Stone was sitting by a log fire, which was giving out a little heat, just enough to take the edge off the cool summer night.

'Mr Stone, you have a guest here. He said you invited him.'

'I did, Colonel Sanquer.'

The ex-soldier stood ramrod straight. 'Please don't bring this club into disrepute.'

'I'm a member here, Sanquer, and I'll thank you to remember that. You're just an employee.'

'But I'll be here long after you're gone,' Sanquer whispered, his voice full of menace.

'Not if you speak to me like that again, fanny baws,' Stone said, feeling his anger rise.

Stone wasn't used to being spoken to like that and was about to get out of his chair when Molloy approached.

'Robert! Please come over and join me.' Stone stood up and they saw there were enough seats for the two Molloys and Jackson.

'We need a seat for Mrs Mellon here,' Michael said. Stone looked at one of the waiters who obliged.

'Drinks will be along shortly, but what can I do for you, Robert?' Stone said.

'We're here because your man was topped this morning.'

'Sad state of affairs, isn't it?' They all sat down as the waiter brought glasses of whisky. Michael looked at his men as they started approaching other guests with the invites for Robert Molloy's new club, one of his men taking a note of who received one.

'This is going to bring unwanted attention onto us, and that is not a thing I like to happen,' Robert said, taking a sip of the whisky. 'And if this is tainted in any way, there will be no Phoenix rising from the ashes of this place.'

'Nobody wants that kind of attention.'

'You think the Hamilton bint is involved?' Michael said.

'That's a bit derogatory, isn't it?' Stone said. 'Considering there's a lady in your company.'

'I wouldn't call Mrs Mellon a bint. She has class.'

'Have you any idea of who would want to kill your architect?' Robert asked.

'You, for a start.'

'Dempsey used to work for me, that's true, and I was pissed off when he jumped ship, but if I'd wanted him topped, you would never have had the opportunity to employ him. Besides, I'm very happy with my new team. Although, you might have decided to have him removed if my plans do win.'

Stone pulled out a cigar and lit it. 'You have a point there, Robert, but I'm a legit businessman. Look at Merchiston. I have plenty of projects on the go. It would be nice to have the New Town North project but not the end of the world if I don't get it.'

'Somebody wanted him dead. And the way they did it, it was like they were sending a message,' Jackson said.

'If it was meant to scare me, then they're going to have a shock coming.'

Greg Sampson, Molloy's head of security, stood off to one side and nodded slightly to Robert.

He stood up, followed by the others. 'Just make sure this doesn't come back to us, George. I can do without the hassle.'

'Good luck on Friday.'

'No luck needed. When is your unveiling again?'

'Next Wednesday, as you well know, since you were invited. I seem to remember telling you a few days ago at Kerry's unveiling.'

'Ah, yes. I forgot.' He looked over at Jackson, who nodded. 'Take care, George. See you around.'

'Same to you, Robert.'

They all left the club, Rita in the middle until they got outside. A minute later, the minibus pulled up and two taxis were hailed.

'Well?' Robert said to Jackson.

'I don't get a feeling about him. I think if he'd wanted Dempsey gone, he'd be in concrete by now, propping up a hotel. But why would Stone want his architect killed?'

'I think you're right.'

'We have to watch our backs, Robert.'

'Goes without saying, my friend.'

FIFTEEN

Andy Watt stepped out of the taxi and couldn't remember the exact location of the flat he was looking for. Then he remembered; right-hand-side of the church, down the stairs to the basement flat.

Bellevue Crescent was in the New Town. Watt knew the area very well after being stationed in Gayfield Square station for a few years.

He was careful going down the stone steps. This was the end of the building and the door was on his right. He hesitated before ringing the bell. He waited, not hearing any movement then all of a sudden, there seemed to be hushed voices, like people whispering, hoping whoever was at the door would go away.

He used the door knocker. 'Open up. Police,' he said.

A minute later, the door opened and a face

appeared. 'I *am* the police,' the man said, then openetl the door wide.

'Fucking hell, Andy,' Paddy Gibb said.

'Do you talk that way to Santa Claus when he comes down your chimney?'

'No. I keep the fire lit. What do you want? It's not bad news, is it? The station's not on fire?'

'Why would that be bad news? Maybe we'd get a modern building that didn't leak warm air in the winter.'

'Again, what's up?'

'I'm not disturbing anything, am I?'

'No, of course not. I was in bed, that's all.' Gibb looked down at the case at Watt's feet. 'Don't tell me you've jacked the job in and you're selling encyclopae-dias? No, wait, I mean, I *do* hope you're selling shite door-to-door, or else that case means something else.'

'Paddy, who is it?' A woman's voice shouted from inside.

'Aw shite,' Gibb said. 'I told her to keep quiet.'

'That's women for you, mate,' Watt said, keeping his voice low in a conspiratorial tone.

'Well, thanks for popping round, Andy, and I'll see you at the station tomorrow.' Gibb made to shut the door.

'She kicked me out, Paddy. And I've already used all my brownie points with my mates.'

'For God's sake. Tell her you're sorry, you love her, and beg for forgiveness.'

'It's not as easy as that; her daughter found the letters that that mad cow from Langholm wrote to me.'

'Ah, Jesus. Didn't I say you should keep it in your pants when we were down there?'

'It was just a fling. I thought Jean was arsing about with other men. Turns out I was wrong.'

'Who is it?' the woman asked again from inside the flat.

'Six months too late for Santa Claus,' Watt said, 'and six months too early for Santa Claus.'

'You've got an unhealthy obsession with Santa.'

'If you spell that another way, you get *Satan*, and that would be even worse.'

The door opened wider as if a gust of wind had blown it and Maggie Parks was standing there, wearing a dressing gown. 'Hello, Andy.'

'Where did you come from?' Gibb said. 'Get out of my house, right now.'

'I don't think Andy's that stupid. Come in, you're letting a draft in.'

Watt picked up his case and entered, while Gibb closed the door behind him. They went through to the living room. 'Beer or coffee?' Maggie said.

'I'll get the kettle on, Mags,' Gibb said, leaving the room.

'What kind of a man puts beer in the kettle?' Watt said.

'This is not a sesh, sergeant,' Gibb shouted back.

'She kicked you out then,' Maggie said. She put a lamp on and switched off the overhead light then sat down.

'Is it that obvious?'

'No, I heard you telling Paddy.'

'Oh, right.'

'Sit down, Andy, you're making the place untidy. Tell me what happened.'

He put the case at the side of the couch. 'I messed up. I slept with a woman while we were in Langholm, despite Paddy's warnings not to. But you should have seen the snow; it was like the end of the world. We were just two lonely people finding solace in each other. I thought we were going to die down there.' He looked at her.

'And you thought you would go out with a bang. Literally.'

'No, not even I believe that.'

'How did Jean find out?'

'This woman's a doctor. You would think she would have had some kind of scruples or something, but no, she started writing to me, and obviously, I didn't show Jean the letters. But Jean's daughter Abi has come to stay and she went snooping through my room.'

'Good God. Why would she do that?'

'Jean and I had hit a rough patch so I was sleeping in the spare room. Abi obviously thought it was fair game to go through my stuff. Anyway, it's over now. She kicked me out and we're finished.'

'Only half-finished, really,' Gibb said, coming back in with some coffees. 'You still have to sort out the bunny boiler.'

'Paddy, that's not very nice,' Maggie said.

'It's true though. She signs the letters, *from your wife.*'

'Oh dear, that does sound a touch possessive. Do you think she's dangerous?'

'I don't want to find out the hard way.'

'How did she find out where you lived?' Gibb asked.

Watt sat in silence for a moment and took a sip of his coffee. 'I have no idea. That's the simple answer. I certainly didn't give her my address.'

'Meantime, you're stuck for somewhere to stay. Thanks for coming to let us know of your predicament. I hope everything works out for you, Andy.' Gibb looked at his watch. 'Is that the time already?'

Maggie looked at him. 'He's your friend, Paddy. Show some compassion.'

'Oh, okay. I'm really sorry that she booted you out, friend.' He paused for a moment. 'Well, goodnight.'

'For God's sake,' Maggie said. 'I know that Andy can be a pain in the arse—'

'Did *he* tell you that?' Watt said.

'Well, you can be, Andy, but I wouldn't see you stuck. At least with me, you get honesty.'

'Fair dos.'

'Do you have anywhere you can go?' Maggie looked genuinely worried.

'Of course he doesn't,' Paddy said. 'That's why he came knocking on my door with his suitcase in hand.' He looked at Watt. 'As much as I'd like to help, I only have one bedroom.'

'No you don't,' Maggie said. 'There's another one through there.'

Gibb's cheeks started going a bit red. 'I meant spare. That's for when the grandkids come over.'

'How often do they spend the night here?'

'Jesus, gang up on Paddy night.'

Watt stood up. 'Look, don't worry about it. I can find a hotel somewhere. Rent a car so I can get to work, as all the hotel rooms in Edinburgh are probably booked by now. Maybe there will be something up in Inverness and I can commute.'

'Oh don't talk pish. Inverness. I'm sure there's something closer – like Dundee.'

'Are you telling me I've been dating a man who

would see his friend out on the street?' Maggie said, standing up.

'Of course not. Andy and I have this banter going. Isn't that right?' He nodded at Watt when Maggie turned away.

'I can't think straight, Paddy. Do we?'

Gibb mouthed *wanker* at him. 'Of course we do. You can take the spare room.'

'For as long as you like,' Maggie said.

'That's fabulous. Thank you both so much. If I haven't said it before, I love you.'

'Don't push it,' Gibb said.

'As long as you don't mention this to anybody, about me and Paddy spending time together. I've practically moved in.'

'My lips are sealed.' Watt picked up his suitcase and held it out for Gibb. 'Be a good lad and put the case through there.'

'Go fu...' Maggie looked at him. '...find it yourself. Down the lobby, second on the right, next to the lav. And I don't want to hear any snoring or farting. Or bringing the bunny boiler home.'

'Aye, aye, Captain.'

'Oh, swanky neighbourhood,' Angel said from the passenger seat. *'Who do you think lives down there?'*

'I have no idea,' Eve Ross said, looking out through the windscreen.

'Maybe you should just go and knock on the door.'

'No, I don't want to do that. Andy's a busy man. He's made the first move though, leaving that bitch. Let's just let him settle into his new place. Give him time to get it nice and cosy.'

'I like that idea. You'll soon be together with him and you can build your life together. But there's one fly in the ointment though, isn't there?'

'Yes, you're right. It has to be taken care of. And it will be. But I have to get it right. I can't just go charging in. I mean, look what happened the last time I tried that.' Eve stared out of the windscreen, from the parking area across the road from the church in Bellevue Crescent.

Across the road from Andy Watt.

She started the car and drove away, her mind planning events that would change both of their lives forever.

'You know I can take care of this for you, don't you?' Angel said.

Eve smiled. 'Yes. I trust you.'

She felt happier than she had felt in months.

SIXTEEN

'I don't give a rat's dick. You think I have spare time to talk to some flat foot?' Kerry Hamilton said. Her personal assistant, Rose, a woman ten years Kerry's senior, raised her eyebrows.

'He's insistent. He says it's important.'

Kerry puffed on her cigarette. The building was no smoking, but considering she owned the building, she made an exception for herself.

'Fuck's sake. We've got a busy time coming up and here we have a copper wanting to sit down and have a cup of tea.'

'You're taking years off your life, Kerry. Those things make you stink.'

'Rose, you do pain me at times. *Stop smoking, Kerry. Cut back on the drinking, Kerry. You'll go blind, Kerry.* What? Are you my mother now?'

'If I was your mother, I'd put you over my bloody knee, young lady.'

Kerry grinned and put the cigarette out. Then gave Rose a hug. 'I wish you had been my mother.'

'That means I would have given birth to you when I was ten.'

'That's it, ruin the image. Disney won't make a movie of my life now.'

'Shall I tell Sherlock Holmes you'll see him now?'

'I suppose. But I meant what I said about me being busy. And I'll only talk to him if you're there.'

'I know you, sweetheart. But just talk to them and get it over with.'

'Fucking Rick Dempsey. What was he doing creeping about in that building anyway?'

'He's George Stone's whipping boy. Probably trying to steal the copper. God knows, Stone would steal anything he could get his hands on.'

'What would I do without you, Rose?'

'Get drunk all the time, go with loose boys, and smoke yourself to death.'

'True. My father says I need to slow things down a bit since I'm approaching forty. Two months away and I won't be able to say I'm in my thirties anymore.'

'Is he still giving you the *When are you going to give me another grandchild* talk?'

'At every opportunity. I told him, I can't be bearing offspring and running your business at the same time.'

'It's your business too, Kerry, don't forget that.'

'I know, but it always seems that it's still father's business. Angela always reminds me of this.'

'Angela should mind her own business and concentrate on producing more grandchildren for your father.'

'I'll tell her that at the next family business meeting.'

Rose laughed. 'They're downstairs. The police.'

'They? I thought you said there was one.'

'It was a generalisation. There's two of them.'

'Good looking?'

'Not bad actually. If there wasn't a Mr Rose, I would be dropping another button.'

'It didn't stop you at last year's Christmas party.'

'That's different, Kerry. The one night a year when we go out and have some fun.'

'Would Mr Rose think the same way?'

'I don't think I'll run that past him. Let's go. You'll have time to talk to the plod and still get to the meeting on time. And no talking about rat's dicks or any other part of their anatomy.'

She stubbed the cigarette out. 'Lead the way. And I hope you took note of me killing that ciggie. I think I just added another ten minutes to my life.'

'Which would mean something if you were in bed

with George Clooney. Right now, it means you can go downstairs and not be stinking of smoke.'

They went down the main staircase to one of the meeting rooms. The two police officers had been shown in and were drinking coffee, chatting amongst themselves until she appeared.

'Gentlemen, thank you for your patience,' she said, not meaning it.

They both stood up. 'I'm Detective Superintendent Purcell, this is Detective Inspector Miller.'

'I'd shake your hand but I know how you men like to go for a piss and not wash your hands afterwards.'

A look passed between both men, as if they had both been caught out and they were each waiting for the other one to come up with a denial.

'We're here to talk about the murder of Rick Dempsey,' Purcell said.

'Really? I thought you were here because you'd seen my profile on a dating site.' She sat down opposite the men, while Rose sat further along. 'I'm kidding, gentlemen, I'm kidding. What can I do you for?'

'We know Mr Dempsey was working for George Stone and there's the competing bids for New Town North, so there is bound to be some conflict.'

'Oh, I see,' Kerry said. 'You think I murdered Dempsey? Or perhaps hired a hitman to kill him?'

'Not at all,' Miller said. 'You people all run around

in the same circles, building flats on every spare piece of land you can get your hands on, so we thought you'd maybe heard something about Dempsey.'

'I heard he liked to drink too much, if that's of any help.'

'We're picking his life apart now, but sometimes somebody will have heard something useful,' Purcell said.

'I haven't heard anything useful about Dempsey,' Kerry answered.

'What about your father?'

'My mother died years ago, and my father decided to retire early from the family business after that. He spends his time on women, drink, and travelling, not necessarily in that order. He keeps his nose in the business but the day-to-day running is left up to me. I make the decisions.'

'We know that all the plans have been submitted after the deadline and there are going to be parties to unveil them,' Purcell said.

'That's correct.'

'Where's yours going to be held?'

'It was at the George Hotel. Monday night. I'm sorry you missed the invite. I'm sure we could have had a good time.'

'Were the other competing teams invited?' Miller asked.

'Yes. We've all been invited to each other's unveiling. Next is Molloy's on Friday night at the dinky little hotel he owns in Prestonfield.'

'Did you know Dempsey to talk to?' Miller said.

'I've met him a few times. Greasy little man. Started to get crude when he had one drink too many. He tried it on with me one time, but my bodyguard sorted him. And by that, I mean he advised Dempsey to sod off. I mean, do I look desperate?'

Miller didn't have any questions after that.

'If there's anything you can help us with, please give us a call,' Purcell said, standing up. He handed her one of his business cards. Miller stood up and they left.

'If anybody was going to top Dempsey, I would think it would be mental Michael Molloy,' she said to Rose after the detectives had gone.

'That boy must have been dropped on his head when he was a baby,' Rose agreed.

'Mind you, I've known Rick Dempsey for a long time now, and I wouldn't trust him to walk past a school playground.'

'You don't think he was a...?'

'Child molester? No, but there *was* something creepy about him. I remember one time we were at a council meeting discussing some plans, and he was creeping about in the corridor. One of the girls at the council said he gave her the chills, and not in a swooning way.'

'Was he married?'

'I think so. But how low does your self-esteem have to be to crawl into bed with the likes of him?'

SEVENTEEN

Dr Harvey Levitt was the force psychologist, a man who talked to officers who had been through traumatic experiences. His main job was working for Edinburgh University. Which is where he met Kim Miller.

'What a pleasant surprise!' he said, his American accent thick.

'I thought you worked over at Infirmary Street?' she said. They were in the building at Teviot Place.

'They keep me in the basement over there, but sometimes they allow me out to wander over here.' He smiled at her. 'What are you doing here?'

'I was talking with a professor from the archaeology department, and a young woman who specialises in cryptology, to see if they could identify some symbols.'

'Any luck?'

She nodded her head. 'Yes.'

'I'm going to the restaurant for a coffee? Care to join me?'

'I'd love to.'

'I'm paying, of course.'

'That's an even better reason.'

When they had their coffees and were sitting at a table away from the groups of students, Levitt asked her: 'How are things with you and Frank?'

'They're fine.'

'They weren't just a little while ago. You coping after finding out about Carol's twin sister?'

'That was a horrendous experience, but at least that chapter is closed now.'

'How's Emma with her new sister?'

'She's wonderful, Harvey. She wants to help with everything, so I make her feel involved.'

'Good. Frank seems to be settling down with you and the girls.'

'He just needed a mental shove.'

He smiled. 'What are these symbols you were asking about, or is it private?'

She reached into her bag and brought out a packet of crime scene photos. She pulled them out and laid them on the table. 'These were drawn in blood near the victim. We couldn't make them out at first because they were drawn in blood, but the cryptologist said it looks like a dog with an Egyptian collar round its neck, which if it is, represents Anubis. He was the God of Death, and he guided people through the underworld.'

'Somebody's telling you that this man was murdered and he's been guided to the underworld. It seems like a warning, if you ask me.'

'A warning?'

'Yes. From a psychological point of view. If whoever killed the man just wanted him dead, they would have murdered him, but the fact they drew these dogs would suggest a warning to whoever found him, or to somebody close to him. Or else, why bother?'

'It could just be a load of hogwash, intended to scare people.'

'Just be on your guard, Kim. From those photos, I can tell somebody was angry.'

'That happens when it's personal. That's why we see murder victims with forty stab wounds or six gunshots to the head, things like that.'

'Overkill,' Levitt said. 'They're punishing the person, even though they're already dead, they have to empty the gun, or keep stabbing until they tire.'

'We know there was more than one. We found two sets of shoe prints in the blood.'

'That sort of changes things.'

'In what way?'

'Rage killings are usually personal, with one person

wanting to hurt the other one so bad. But with two, it's a whole new ball game. Torture, execution. Sending a message. Whoever it is, they're not messing about.'

'I know. It's scary what people can do to each other.' Kim shivered and thought about her two daughters. And wondered how old they would be when they realised just what sort of a world they lived in.

EIGHTEEN

The house was a bungalow at Craigleith. Miller had dropped Purcell off as he had a meeting to go to, and Watt had jumped into the passenger seat of Police Scotland's version of the Batmobile.

Rick Dempsey had worked hard but didn't splash his money about. His wife's eyes were red from crying and she kept grabbing a tissue from the box in front of her and wiping her eyes.

Miller and Andy Watt were sitting opposite her.

'Even the car outside is a Ford. Rick didn't like to spend money on frivolous things. The house was our biggest expenditure, but he wouldn't sink money into cars that were going to lose half their value as soon as you drove them off the forecourt. That car out there is shared, or was shared, by both of us and it was used when we bought it.'

'Did you know anybody who would have wanted to harm him, Mrs Dempsey?' Miller asked her.

Mrs Dempsey started crying again and another woman, Ellen Reid, who had introduced herself as her sister, came back into the living room with another pot of tea.

'This is just a travesty. Rick wouldn't have done anything to hurt a fly. I hope you people are doing all you can to find his killer.'

'That's why we're here,' Watt said, beginning to be irritated by the woman.

'They still haven't told us how he died,' she said, pouring from the teapot.

'It's fine, Nettie. Don't take it out on them, they're only doing their job.'

'I'll leave you to it, but I'll be through in the kitchen if you need me.'

'Can you tell us about your family?' Miller said.

'Toby, he's twenty-three, lives in London now. He's an architect like his dad. Mary is twenty-one, going into her last year of university. She wants to be an engineer. They were both away when Rick was murdered.'

'So, nobody annoyed at your husband?' Watt said.

'We lived a quiet life. Rick threw himself into his work. George Stone kept him busy. More so these days since Stone was working on that new project.'

'The New Town North one?'

'No, the other one. Out in Penicuik. It was more of a secret project. Sort of. Rick just said that he couldn't talk about it much, but he was excited.'

'Is Stone building more houses out there?' Watt said.

'I have no idea. The only thing Rick said was, it was secret.'

'Did your husband have any gambling debts, anything like that?'

'No. You couldn't have met a nicer man. He went to work and came home to his family. We were married for nearly thirty years, and as far as I'm aware, he wasn't having an affair. God knows why anybody would want to kill him.'

Miller knew he was getting nowhere, and after a few more minutes, stood up ready to leave. 'Thank you for your time, Mrs Dempsey. If you think of anything, please give me a call.'

Ellen saw Miller out. She indicated for him to step outside and she pulled the door gently closed behind her so they were both standing out in the sunshine.

'He *was* having an affair, the bastard,' Ellen said.

'Really? Mrs Dempsey didn't think to seem so. What makes you so sure?'

'I saw him with another woman, twice. Having a drink. They looked very comfortable with each other.'

'She might have been a friend,' Watt said.

'Aye, and I'll be riding a unicorn home. She was more than a friend, I was sure of it.'

'Are you not sure now?' Miller was starting to feel confused by the woman.

'The opposite. I know for a fact. I hired a private investigator to follow him and he got photos of them going into a hotel. They were in there for hours. He got photos of them leaving.'

'Do you know who this woman is?' Watt said.

'Not yet. But I got a photo of them sitting in a café. Mobile phones are marvellous these days. You can pretend to be talking to somebody on the phone while you've actually switched the sound off and you've taken a photo of them without them knowing. Here, I'll show you. This was taken just a couple of weeks ago.' Ellen fished her phone out of her trouser pocket and brought up the photo album and showed them Rick Dempsey with the woman.

Jean Melrose.

Miller asked for the name of the investigator before they walked away. Andy Watt was stunned into silence.

'I told you,' was all he would say to Miller.

NINETEEN

Robert Molloy was in his sixties and didn't mind having a drink or two at the weekend, but a Thursday night was usually reserved for kicking back in his house in Heriot Row. He was thinking about using an online dating app.

'They're all the same on these sites,' his son Michael said. 'All they're looking for a is a good seeing to.'

'And?'

'Your ticker won't take it.'

'Shut up. What are you doing round here anyway?'

Michael sat down on a couch after pouring two whiskies and passing one to his father. 'I just wanted to go over everything for tomorrow night.'

'What's to go over? The catering is sorted, and the model is being kept secret and will be delivered under guard. The RSVPs are in so we know who's coming. Everything's taken care of.'

'I think we should have extra men there.'

'Michael, don't get your Ys in an uproar. Adrian is supplying the extra men.'

'I hope they're not a bunch of fucking yahoos. Weekend warriors who go around pretending they were in special forces.'

'They're not, they're the real deal. You don't think I would take Jackson's word for it, do you?'

'This coming from the man who is trying to snag a piece online.'

'Piece? For fuck's sake. I'm looking for a companion, not some fucking crack whore.'

'Jesus, you could get any woman you want. Some young thing in her late twenties would do it.'

'I'm not looking to die on top of her, I'm looking for somebody who I can have a conversation with. Have a meal, watch a film with.'

'When's the last time you went to the pictures?'

'I meant in here on Netflix or something.'

'There are plenty of sites nowadays; everything from midgets to grannies. Take your pick.'

'God Almighty, does your girlfriend know you talk like this?'

'She knows I'm the perfect gentleman,' Michael said, finishing his whisky.

'If you were the perfect gentleman, you would have put a ring on her finger by now.'

Michael looked at his father. 'It's hard after being married before and knowing she was murdered.'

Robert looked solemn. 'I know, son. I loved her too.' He finished his own whisky. 'Right, bugger off, I have company coming round. She'll be here any minute.'

'Anybody I know?'

'No, and I have no intention of introducing her to you.'

'Nice. Your only son and you don't want to show me off. Anybody would think you kept me in the attic.' He stood up.

'Is your driver outside?'

'He is. He's a good guy. And the others are at the house with Liz. After that fiasco with that woman, I'm not taking any chances.'

'Wise choice.' Robert got up and saw his son out the front door and looked at his watch. His guest was late, which didn't sit too well with him.

He watched as Michael got into the back of the Lexus and the car glided away. He saw a woman walking towards his house.

Molloy sensed somebody standing at the kitchen door further along the hallway and turned to see one of his guards there.

'Would you like the coffee machine on, sir?'

'No thanks. We'll be in the den.'

He turned back to look out and the woman was walking up the outside steps. She smiled up at him. He stepped to one side and let her in.

'Hello, Robert,' Jean Melrose said.

'Come in.' He smiled at her and his assistant – even Molloy was embarrassed to call him his butler – stepped forward and took Jean's coat.

'I thought we could have a bite to eat in the den. You hungry?'

'I am a bit, although my stomach has been turning flips after what just happened.'

'Don't you worry your sweet little head over that, my dear.'

The guard was still standing at the doorway to the kitchen and Molloy nodded to him; *go and get the champagne.*

The den was a spacious room much like the living room but it had a large TV at one end, and a new pool table that Molloy had recently bought.

'You fancy watching some mindless movie on Netflix?'

'Yes, why not?'

'My housekeeper is rustling us up some supper. We can eat then watch something.'

'Thank you for letting me come over. I can imagine

just how busy you are, what with the presentation tomorrow.'

'There's nothing else to prepare for. Michael's handling a lot of the stuff. I was at a loose end anyway. All I had planned was a few games of pool. My guard – who's the housekeeper's husband – and I have a wee tournament going on. The bugger's beating me.'

'What does he get if he wins?' She grinned at him.

'Ten grand.'

'Ten grand? You must pay him a lot.'

'You asked what *he* gets if he wins. Ten grand. If I win, I get a tenner. It's the winning that counts not taking part. Something like that.'

The housekeeper wheeled in a trolley.

'Please sit down, Jean,' Molloy said. He held her chair for her while she sat. Then he sat and they watched as the lid was lifted on the stainless-steel serving dishes.

'Steak and the trimmings,' he said. He thanked the woman and she retreated as her husband came in with the champagne and poured two glasses.

When they were alone, he clinked glasses with her. 'I feel like a fraud, Robert. Unless this is going to be my last supper.'

Molloy tutted. 'Jean, how long have we known each other now? Too many years to remember. I respect you and can assure you that this is not your fault.'

'It is in a way.'

Molloy cut a piece of steak and held it on his fork. 'Not at all. I won't have you talking this way.'

'We had an agreement and it all went up in a puff of smoke.' She cut into her own meat.

'Nonsense. To be honest, I'm surprised it lasted as long as it did.'

'Me too. But Rick was a nice guy. I liked him a lot.'

'He was a twat. Tell me the full story of how it went pear-shaped with Watt.'

'You know I have a daughter?' she said.

He nodded and tucked into his meal.

'She went to live with her father in London ten years ago. Long story short, she wanted to come back up here after her father died, and I said yes. Andy took an instant dislike to her and she made it clear she didn't like him either. Turns out, when Andy was away in that Borders town, Langholm, he met somebody else and slept with her. Then she apparently started writing him letters. This woman is in love with him.'

'He left you for her?'

'Oh no. And this is where it gets messy; I kicked him out. And that's why I feel so bad. It's over between us and now I can't give you any more information.'

Molloy swallowed some more meat and washed it

down with the champagne. 'Don't you worry about that. It wasn't going to last forever. I don't think Watt would have asked you for your hand in marriage. If he was going to, he would have done so by now.'

'I'm glad he didn't. That would have been awful, turning him down.'

'We both got something out of this, Jean. And I can't thank you enough. You did a good job with Dempsey, but now that he's dead, it's finished. But you and I will still be working together. And I will be buying more and more property in this city.'

'Good God, Robert, it seems that every spare piece of land is being built on. One day there's a petrol station, the next there's a block of flats on it. It's happening all over the place. But that's nice to know.'

'I know. And we don't have to put any scare tactics on people in order for them to sell up. There's an absolute mint to be made on places now. Especially in decent areas. And I want you to be there, along for the ride. Decent interior designers are hard to come by. Some of the ones that Stone uses must be sniffing glue.'

'I don't deserve this, Robert.'

'Nonsense! You did what was asked of you, and I got something out of it too. We make good partners, Jean.'

She smiled. 'I'll drink to that.'

TWENTY

Jean Melrose sat back in the taxi and had to admit that she missed Andy already. Then the anger kicked in when she remembered what he had done. *You're the one who was working with Robert Molloy!* They had both done something behind the other's back, but she tried to convince herself that what she had done was the best for her. It had been the best for her business.

Years ago, her husband had walked out, leaving her high and dry. She had a little girl to feed, and instead of going on government handouts, she had fought her way back. She had built up her business and was successful.

Meeting Andy Watt online had been fun. She'd been at a low point in her life, and he was handsome and funny and good company.

Then she had been invited to dinner by her old

friend, Robert Molloy. He had made her a proposal; liaise with Rick Dempsey and he would see to it that she would have the contract as interior designer for the places he was buying and refurbishing, or having built from scratch.

Too many nights lying awake, wondering if her business was going to survive, made her jump at the chance. And she had made a small fortune from Molloy.

And of course, she had kept her end of the bargain. George Stone would not have been a happy camper if he had known that Dempsey was feeding information to Molloy via her.

She got the taxi driver to drop her off round the corner from her house, in Pentland Avenue. She wanted to see if Andy was hanging about, waiting to see if he could persuade her to let him back. *Let's sit down and talk.* That's what her ex had done. Begged her to take him back after he had been cheating on her. She had told him to his face to go blow himself.

She didn't think Andy would do that, but you could never tell what somebody was going to do when they wanted a different outcome from the one you were giving them.

It was warm with a slightly chilly undertone. She was wearing a lightweight jacket and pulled the collar together. This was a quiet area, and she walked round into her own street but didn't see any cars parked near her driveway.

She felt foolish. Whatever Andy was, he wasn't some obsessive stalker.

She heard the slightest brush of a shoe on the pavement behind her. Her heart bumped up a gear and she started to turn round just before something hit her hard on the head and she collapsed to the ground.

Then the feet started kicking her, and a boot caught her in the face. All she saw was a figure standing over her before blackness took over.

TWENTY-ONE

'Is Maggie coming round tonight?' Watt said. He was in Gibb's kitchen, raking about in the fridge for a couple of beers.

'Not while you're going about the place practically naked.'

Watt looked at him. 'I have a dressing gown on. I'm going for a shower in a minute. I'm not a complete animal.' He grabbed a couple of bottles and handed one to Gibb. 'I bought these earlier. I didn't want you to think I'm taking advantage of your hospitality.'

'Just remember and put a new bog roll on the holder when you use the last bit.'

'I will. But is Mags coming round? If she is, I can make myself scarce.'

'Well, as we're just friends, and she sometimes pops in for coffee—'

Watt put up a hand. 'Did you bang your nut this morning? I saw her parading about here in her dressing gown. Unless she sleepwalks like that, I'm fully aware of what you two get up to. I've known about the birds and bees for a long time.'

'We just don't want it spread around the station.'

'I won't say a word. You're good enough to rent me out your spare room.... I mean, let me kip here for a couple of nights, so you have my word.'

'Wait a minute. Back that up a bit. Rent out a room?'

'Relax, Paddy. I'll be here for a few days, tops.'

'I told you not to touch that woman down in Langholm, didn't I?' He drank some of the cold beer.

'My big brain was saying, *Don't do it, you arsehole.* The small one was saying, *Go on, nobody will ever find out.* You know what it's like; the wee brain has no conscience. I got carried away, that's all.'

'Thinking with your nob. Try putting the big brain in gear next time.'

'Is this a fling with you and Maggie?' Watt asked as they went through to the living room.

'To be honest, I don't know. I can't see myself going the long haul with her, so we're just taking each day as it comes.'

'Well, here's to us. I hope everything works out for you.' They clinked beer bottles.

Then Watt's mobile phone rang. It was Frank Miller.

'What's going on, Frank?'

'I have some bad news, Andy. Where are you?'

Andy and Gibb were sitting at the kitchen table when Miller came in with Jeni Bridge and Percy Purcell. He'd put clothes on.

'I didn't realise Paddy had thrown a surprise party,' said Andy.

'Could we go through to the living room while they talk, Paddy?' said Purcell.

Paddy stood and followed Purcell out of the room.

Miller looked at Andy without smiling. 'Andy, I'm going to ask you something, and I know we've known each other for a long time, so don't take it personally; where were you two hours ago?'

'What's this about?'

'Just answer the question,' Jeni said.

'I was here, having a few beers with Paddy. Why?'

'Where were you earlier tonight?' Purcell said to the DCI once Paddy was seated in the living room.

'I've been in all evening. Andy and I were having a few beers. Why?'

'He didn't leave at all?'

'No, we were having a drink. Neither of us left.'

Purcell nodded and left the room and went back into the kitchen.

'Is somebody going to tell me what this is all about? And remember I'm a copper too so no crap.'

'Jean was attacked earlier tonight. She's alive but they've put her in an induced coma,' Jeni said.

Wat suddenly stood up. 'Jesus Christ. I have to go and see her.'

'Easy there, Andy. It won't do any good, and Professional Standards have told us you haven't to go near her.'

'Fuck standards. If I want to go see her, then I'll go and see her.'

'No you won't, sergeant,' Purcell said. 'If you go near the Royal, you'll be suspended.'

'Where did it happen?' Watt said.

'Outside her house.'

'In her street? Jesus, that's an upscale neighbourhood.'

'People travel,' Miller said.

'What did they do to her?'

'The doctors think she was kicked. There's part of a boot print on her face.'

'Fuck me. Was it a robbery?'

'No,' Purcell said, 'nothing was taken.'

'Who the hell would want to hurt her? And thanks

for thinking it was me.' He knew he was being unfair; they knew he had split with her and he was the prime suspect until his alibi held up.

'We're going through the motions, Andy,' Miller said. 'If we thought you were guilty of it, we would have come in here and taken you to the station.'

'Point taken. But do you have anything to go on?'

'Not yet. There are no witnesses. Even the taxi driver who dropped her off didn't see anything.'

'Where was she picked up?' Watt asked.

'In Howe Street, leading up from Stockbridge. It's a route taxis take to get back into the centre of town. A man flagged down a taxi and Jean got out of the back of a Range Rover and the man got into it after Jean got in the taxi.'

'That's strange. I wonder who she was with?'

'It was a young man,' Jeni said.

'She moved on quickly enough.' Andy Watt said it with a matter of fact tone.

'We're not here to question her personal decisions,' Jeni said. 'but to ascertain who attacked her. When we get him, he'll be charged with attempted murder.'

Or her, Andy thought but didn't voice it.

'Right, we'll leave you to it, sergeant,' Purcell said. 'But heed the warning; no going to the Royal.'

'I'm assuming you've spoken to her daughter?'

'Oh, yes. Why do you think we came here?' Jeni

left with Purcell while Miller stayed. When the other two officers were gone, Gibb came through from the living room and got Miller a beer from the fridge.

'Sorry to hear that news,' he said.

'Thank God you were together,' Miller said.

'Christ, don't say it like that, Frank. I mean, I'm in the spare room.'

'I'm not meaning anything by it. But if you had been alone in a wee bedsit or something, they would have had your balls nailed to the wall. But we have to address the eight-hundred-pound elephant in the room.'

Watt took a swig of the beer. 'Eve Ross.'

'Exactly. We suspect she's in Edinburgh because of the postmark, so if she is here, then we have to assume she could have gone to Jean's address as that was where the letters were sent. She knew where you lived.'

Gibb lit up a cigarette. 'I hope she was a good ride. I would hate to think she's popped a cog in her head and she was shite in bed. I mean, it bodes well for when you're married to her.'

'God Almighty, that doesn't bear thinking about. Besides, she did confess that she fancied you as well.'

'That *will* be fucking right.' Gibb lit up a cigarette. 'She better not show her face round here.'

'She doesn't know I'm here.'

'She didn't know where you lived in Edinburgh, but she still found out,' Miller said.

'That's it, give me the willies,' Gibb said.

'That's what she said.'

'Anyway,' Miller said, 'they'll be checking out any CCTV in the area where she got into the taxi, to see if somebody was watching or followed the taxi. Do you know if she has CCTV outside her house?'

Watt shook his head. 'No. It's pretty secure. She didn't bother with any of that. There's a camera above her garage, but it's a dummy. Me? I'd have a fucking Dobermann that would rip your nuts off.'

'Not in here,' Gibb said.

'Of course not; you have...' Gibb shot him a look just as he was about to say, *Maggie*. '...a nice place you don't want ruined by a dog. Puking on the carpet. Mind you do that as well when you're blootered, so nobody would know any difference.' Then he thought about Jean lying in a hospital bed, in a coma, and his banter fell away.

'I'll do anything I can to find the bastard who did this. Even though we'll never be together again, I owe her this.'

The others lifted their beer bottles and they clinked them together.

TWENTY-TWO

The store front was a barber's shop, and Andy Watt thought he'd got the wrong place at first.

'Help you?' the old barber said to him, pausing mid cut.

'I was looking for Phoenix Private Investigators. I thought this was the address.' He made to go.

'Through there,' the old man said, pointing to a narrow corridor at the back of the shop. Watt walked along it and saw a couple of doors. One had glass in it with the name etched in gold on the pane. He opened the door and walked in. A woman sat at a desk. She smiled at him.

'I'm here to see Bruce Hagan. I'm Andy Watt. I called ahead.'

'Oh yes. My name's Shirley. I'm the brains of the firm. Starsky and Hutch are through the back. I'll let them know you're here.' She turned slightly. 'Bruce! Company.'

Watt winced at the sound of the woman's voice.

The door to the back office opened. 'I told you before, Shir, we have an intercom,' Hagan said.

Shirley was larger than life and so was her laugh.

'I don't suppose there's any chance of a coffee?' he asked.

'Oh, honey, as much as I'd love to run after you like an eighteenth-century wench, I'm afraid I have some typing to do.' She looked at Watt. 'I count myself lucky he spent money on a computer and not a typewriter.'

'Come on through, Andy,' Hagan said. Watt stepped past the desk and went into the office. It was larger than he'd thought it was going to be.

'Sit down,' Hagan said, pointing to a client chair.

'No coffee then?' Watt said.

'Bloody kettle went tits up and fanny out there refuses to leave to go to the coffee place round the corner.' He sat down. 'What brings you here, Andy?'

'I appreciate you seeing me, Bruce. I have a problem that I thought I'd run by you and see if you can help me fix it.'

'That's what I get paid for. But since it's for you, I'll give you the *Lothian and Borders* special.'

'Not something you have to give out all that often, I imagine.'

'You're the first. I'll have to get a certificate made up.'

'I heard Percy Purcell's old man works for you.'

'He does,' Hagan said, leaning back in the office chair. 'He's an asset. We get on really well.' He was wearing a cotton glove, covering the fact he had lost some fingers. There was silence for a second, almost like Watt was a suspect sitting across from Hagan. A window overlooked a small close behind the barber shop.

They heard a toilet flush and Lou Purcell came in.

'Lou, this is DS Andy Watt. He works on your dad's team.'

'Hi, Andy. If you're here to arrest us, he made me do it.'

'No, I'm here on private business.'

'Great.' He sat down on another chair.

'What can we help you with, Andy?' Hagan said.

'This is difficult for me, but here we go; I was on a case in Langholm a few months ago. I had a little one-night stand with a woman. Now she's writing letters, and saying she wants to be with me. My girl-friend found out and kicked me out and I just want to know if you can find something out about this woman. Maybe go to Langholm and see what her colleagues think of her. Just some snooping about.'

He leaned forward. 'We can do that, eh, Lou?'

'We certainly can.'

'I can pay you the going rate.'

'Andy, we worked together. I don't want money from you.'

'Uh oh. I get the feeling I'm going to be getting shafted.'

'Not at all. But I can do this and all I ask in return is that you could maybe look up some things for me.' Hagan was expecting to hear an argument.

'Okay, done. But don't expect to get a direct line into the station.'

'Fine. Just now and again when I get stuck on something.'

'Fine by me.'

'Give me the details and I'll get going on it,' Hagan said.

Watt brought out a few sheets of paper and the pile of letters. Read some of them. You'll get an idea of what I'm up against.'

Hagan nodded and opened the first one and read it. He put it down.

'Well?' Watt said.

'I think I can't get to Langholm fast enough, my friend.'

'Listen, mate, I know there's confidentiality with these cases, but I need you to help me with something else if you can.'

'Fire away.'

'You were on a job, following a man whose wife thought he was cheating. He was photographed with a woman. That woman was my girlfriend. Would you be able to shed any light on it?' said Andy.

'Normally, I'd have to say no, but you helped me a lot when I was on the force. Let me see. What's his name?'

'Rick Dempsey.'

Hagan played with the computer keyboard. 'As I said, normally I couldn't, but considering she was your girlfriend.' He looked at Watt. 'No. I couldn't find any evidence of an affair. They always met in a public space, talked, and then parted ways. If they went to a hotel, then they must have been very clever about it. As far as I can see, all they ever did was talk.'

TWENTY-THREE

Miller was with Hazel Carter. Hazel was driving, and they pulled up outside Jean's house.

'Andy landed on his feet when he met Jean Melrose,' Hazel said.

'And threw it all away again,' Miller said, looking at the house. 'And for some nutter he met when we were at Langholm.'

'You were with him there. Did you meet her?'

'Of course. She worked with us.'

'Did she seem normal to you?'

'What's normal? Maybe she thought we were the nutters. Andy slept with her and in her mind, that meant they were going to be joined at the hip.'

They got out of the car and walked up to the front door. Miller rang the doorbell and they waited a few minutes until somebody answered. Instead of Jean's daughter who they were expecting to see, a young man answered.

'If you're from the papers, we can give you a story, but it's going to cost you.'

They held out their warrant cards. 'You are?'

'Oh, Mark. I'm Abi's friend.'

'Well, Abi's friend, do you think we could come in?' Hazel said.

'Abi's not here.'

'That's okay. We'd still like to talk to you.'

Mark stepped aside and let them in. The hallway was cool, with a tiled floor and a centre staircase. Hallways led off on both sides and Mark led them through to a living room.

'No TV?' Miller said.

'There's a separate TV room. And a theatre room. And—'

'I was being facetious,' Miller said.

'Oh. Right. Find a seat.'

The detective looked around the room and saw newspapers lying about, fast food wrappers on the floor. No signs of drug use but Miller thought that might be evident in another room.

'What can I help with?' Mark said.

Miller and Hazel moved some magazines and sat on a couch. 'Abi Melrose's mother was attacked out here last night and we want to ask you some questions about that.'

'Whoa, whoa,' Mark said, leaning forward in the big leather chair. 'I had nothing to do with that. Do I need a lawyer?'

'Not unless you want to. We can talk down at the station if you like?' Hazel said.

'Whoa, whoa,' Mark said again. 'Let's not get our panties twisted here. I was only asking.'

'Where were you last night?' Miller said.

Mark looked up at the ceiling. Blew out his breath. Took his time thinking about it before bringing his eyes back down to earth. 'Here.'

'Not in outer space, then?' Hazel said.

'Nope.'

'Were you here alone?'

'Nope.'

'Who were you with? And if you answer with *nope*, well, let's just say it's that time of the month and I will chew you a new fucking arsehole.'

'Who...' he started to say but thought better of it. 'Listen to *her*,' Mark said to Miller as if Hazel couldn't hear. 'You have to go about with her all day?'

Miller stood up. 'I think this interview would be better conducted down at the station.'

'No, no, I'll answer your questions. I'm just a bit... tired.'

'You should take something for that, then,' Hazel said. 'Something to help you sleep.'

Mark laughed and pointed to her.

Then a young woman came into the room and looked at the detectives before looking at Mark. *Polis,* he whispered.

'You are?' Miller said.

'Lynn... Rogers,' Lynn Bridge said, using her mother's maiden name. 'I'm Mark's girlfriend.'

'Were you here last night when Jean Melrose was attacked outside?' Miller said.

'I was here with Mark and Abi. We didn't hear anything. We were listening to music.'

'Do you both live here?' Hazel asked.

'Yes,' Mark answered.

'How long?'

'Not long. We just moved in,' Lynn said, still standing.

'You didn't know Jean well then?'

'We're friends of Abi. Her mother was okay with us moving in. The house is big and we're in the separate wing.'

'Did you ever hear Jean arguing with anybody?'

'No, never.'

'Did you see anybody hanging about outside?' Hazel said.

'No,' Lynn said.

'Nope,' Mark said, then shot a glance at Hazel.

There was silence for a moment before Miller stood up. 'Thanks for your help.'

Hazel stood up and looked at Mark for a few seconds before he looked away, then they left the house.

'Christ, did you see that? He's high on something.'

'And you still managed to put the fear of death into him. Time of the month talk.'

'It's not really. I just felt hacked off this morning.'

They got back in the car and Miller rolled his window down, letting some of the warm air out. 'One thing's strange though.'

'What's that?' Hazel asked.

'That girl. She said her name is Lynn Rogers. That's not her name. Unless she got married recently, but I think we would have heard about that.'

'Do you know her?'

'I've seen her photo on Jeni Bridge's desk. That's her daughter.'

TWENTY-FOUR

'It's been years since I was down in the Borders,' Lou Purcell said as they entered Langholm.

'Me too. Not since I was a kid.' Bruce Hagan looked at the older man from the passenger seat. 'The police station is part of the town hall according to Andy Watt.'

Lou went round the back of the building to where the little car park was. They got out into the late morning sunshine.

'It must have been wicked in that snowstorm,' Lou said. 'The bridges into town were knocked down. A petrol tanker crashed and exploded it was that bad.'

They went into the cool of the old building and walked up to the public counter.

'How can I help you?' the big, burly sergeant said.

'I'm Bruce Hagan, this is Lou Purcell. We're

looking for Sergeant Dan Brown.' Both men showed ID.

'Then you've found him,' Brown said.

'Good. We spoke on the phone. You said you could give me some information on Dr Eve Ross.'

Brown eyed them with suspicion for a moment. 'There's not much I can tell you about her, but if you go across the road to the Thomas Hope hospital, maybe some of her colleagues there will be able to help.'

After pointing them in the right direction, they walked over to the hospital. It was a small affair, the building built back in the eighteen hundreds.

Inside, Hagan walked up to a receptionist and told her what they wanted. She made a call and a nurse manager came out to see them and took them into an office.

'We were sorry to lose her,' the woman said, 'but you understand I can't discuss too much about her time here, due to privacy issues. Is there something wrong?'

'She's missing. Somebody has employed us to look for her. Somebody who's very worried about her.'

'I didn't think she had any family.'

'It's her husband to be.'

Lou kept a straight face and didn't look at Hagan, in a well-rehearsed move that they'd talked about in the car on the way down.

It's not a lie, Hagan had said, *she signs the letters, your wife.*

'Oh my goodness. I didn't realise.'

'You can imagine how worried he is,' Lou said.

'Oh yes, I can.'

'You might know him,' Hagan continued, 'his name is Andy Watt. He's a police officer in Edinburgh. They met here, and she was going to go to Edinburgh to be with him, but as far as he knows, she didn't make it. And being a police officer, they're doing everything they can up there, but they've achieved nothing so far. Detective Watt asked me, as a former colleague, to help out. That's why we're here.'

'Oh, this is awful. She was so happy. I remember her talking about going to Edinburgh, but she didn't say too much. I know she had handed in her notice a few weeks ago, something like that. And I'm not breaking any privacy rules by telling you that. However, she was good friends with Morag Cowan. She's an assistant at the Julie Dumbarton art gallery, just down the road. You should go and talk to her.'

Hagan thanked her, and she wrote the address down for them. It was within walking distance, just further south.

'She sounds like a right nut-bag, this Ross woman,' Lou said.

'Is that your professional opinion, Dr Purcell?'

'It is indeed.'

'I concur with that diagnosis. Let's go and see if we can find this female friend of the good doctor.'

The art gallery was in an old church, on Drove Road, halfway up a hill. It had a small private car park in front.

'Looks like the old minister got a parking space but the parishioners had to hoof it,' Lou said.

'There are quite a few churches in Langholm but maybe only a couple used for their intended purpose.'

'At least this one got saved,' a voice said from behind them. 'You must be Hagan and Purcell.'

'The smoke signals at work?' Lou said.

'Mobile phones. I knew you were here before you even hit the Thomas Hope, but the director called me and gave me a heads-up. Let's go in, have a cup of coffee. I'm just back from lunch but I'm always up for a coffee.'

'Morag Cowan?' Hagan said.

'The very one.'

She unlocked the front door and they went inside. What was once the main part of the church was now the studio. The lack of pews made the interior seem like a gigantic cathedral in Lou's eyes.

'Been a long time since I set foot in a church. And

it wasn't as nice as this one.' Two tall stained-glass windows flanked a smaller, round one, high up on the end wall. The ceiling was painted red while the walls were white, bringing a modern feel to the building. A large table sat in the middle, covered in paint brushes and paints.

'You won't find absolution in this one, Mr Purcell. You will definitely find some outstanding paintings by a local artist though.'

'This is some spectacular work,' Hagan said, looking around. Large original Julie Dumbarton paintings hung on the walls. Easels were off to one side. A table sat against one wall with a wooden kitchen chair at it, as if it was waiting patiently for the occupant to come back.

'I think Julie would be pleased to hear that,' Morag said. 'Come through to the back and I'll get the kettle on.'

They followed her along a short corridor to the back and found themselves in a small kitchen.

'This would have made a nice house,' Lou said.

'Wouldn't it just? Fortunately, this old building was bought and given a new lease of life.'

They sat and chatted while the kettle boiled. Coffees made, they sat at the table.

'I believe you're looking for Eve?'

'Yes, she's missing.'

'That is sad news. I do hope she's alright. Any idea of what happened to her?'

'She was supposed to meet up with a friend of ours. Andy Watt. Eve might have spoken of him.'

'Andy! Yes, Eve spoke non-stop about him.'

'He's worried,' Lou said.

'Aren't the police doing anything?'

'As I said to the nursing director, the police sometimes go through the motions. I should know, I was one of them. But to be fair, there's only so much they can do. Eve is a doctor, she's an adult, and if she wants to disconnect herself from people, it's not a crime. But because Andy's so worried about her, he asked us to look into it.'

'Oh, he's such a caring man. I'm sure he'll be a good friend as well as a husband.'

Lou kept a straight face. 'I'm sure he will.'

'Unlike poor Simon.'

'Simon?' Bruce said.

'Professor Simon Larking. He was head pathologist down in Dumfries and Galloway.'

'Was he an ex of hers or something?'

'Oh, no. He was just a friend. But the way he died.'

Hagan sat forward. 'Do you mind if I ask what happened?'

'Well, I can tell you because it was in all the papers.' She looked uncertain for a moment before she carried on.

'He hanged himself.'

TWENTY-FIVE

'I'm telling you, I was that fucking close to lamping Jackson one,' Davy Dickson said, holding his thumb and index finger half an inch apart.

'Don't fucking let him hear you talk like that.'

'Talking to me like that,' Dickson said, carrying on as if he hadn't heard. 'Coming back to Edinburgh, throwing his weight about. Next time, I might just give him a rectal exam with that fucking sword of his. I mean, who wears a bowler hat? Seriously.'

Crawley's mobile phone rang and he answered it. 'Yes, Mr Jackson. Davy is right here. I'll get him for you.' Crawley held the phone away from his face. 'He says he has our flat bugged and he wants to know why you're bad-mouthing him.'

'Eh? Away to fuck.' Dickson's face lost its colour.

'Of course he doesn't, twat. He probably just wants

to go over what we're doing tonight.' He held the phone out for Dickson to take.

Dickson grabbed it.

'Fucking snatch it,' Crawley complained as Dickson put the phone to his ear.

'This is Davy, Mr Jackson.'

'Are you two pair of reprobates ready for tonight?'

'Yes, Mr Jackson. In fact, Des and I were just going over things before you called.' He turned round and stuck two fingers up at Crawley. 'And we're wearing black just like you said.'

'Is creepy drawers ready to go?'

'Yes, sir. We're both dressed and ready to leave.' Dickson looked down at himself; he was still in his vest and underpants, as was Crawley. He made a moving motion with his hand, indicating for Crawley to get a move on.

'Don't let me down, Dickson. And no drinking, or you'll never be able to lift another pint glass again. Understood?'

'Crystal clear, sir.' He listened for a moment longer as the phone was disconnected on the other end.

'Did you tell him we're two, finely-tuned machines that are preparing to go to work? I mean, you wouldn't just jump into a Ferrari and boot the bollocks off it without letting the oil warm up first,' Crawley said.

'I'll convey that message to him, next time we see him.'

'He better be putting his hand deep into his pocket for this. I mean, talk about going above and beyond.'

'He's asked us to do a job. We had a job, remember? And we screwed it up.'

'We? You were the one getting pished every night and sleeping in the van.'

'We're a team, Des. There's no I in *team*.'

'There's no I in *wanker* either.'

'The blame is on us, not just me.'

'Christ, he's asking us to break into a house. It's the not the same as falling asleep on the job.'

'Are ye daft? He wants us to snoop around and look for some papers. You think we're going to leave with just papers? We'll be having a sniff around and swipe what we can. Like it's a bonus.'

Crawley smiled. 'I like it.'

'That's why they pay me the big bucks.'

'What do you mean?'

'I don't know,' Dickson said, 'I heard it on TV.'

'Right,' Crawley said, standing up, 'we better get ready. Then tomorrow when me meet him, you can give him a good boot in the bowler hat.'

'Any of them take your fancy?' Rose asked.

Kerry Hamilton looked around the ballroom of the Holyrood Park Hotel with a look on her face like she was chewing a piece of meat a dog had spat out. 'Rose, don't you know me by now? I mean, would you take your dress off for any of them?'

'No, but I'm married. You, young lady, are looking for a beau. That's what you told me.'

'Beau? Jesus, Rose. I'm not looking for a young stud, I'm looking for an octogenarian with a bad ticker.'

'You don't need money.'

'No, I don't, but I wouldn't say no to more of it.'

'Instead of waking up to a young stud, you'd rather wake up to old age creeping up on you.'

'Precisely. I don't want some guy to go out with me because I have money. I mean, what if he tries to take advantage of me, Rose?'

'First of all, your personal bodyguard, Travis, is a former marine, and I would cause him pain in parts of his body he didn't even know existed.'

Kerry smiled. 'I love you, Rose.'

'Don't say that out loud in front of a prospective beau.'

'Check.'

A man who looked to be in his fifties approached. 'Hello, my name's Stuart. Can I get you a drink?'

'Is *Stuart* short for *Dick?*' Rose said.

'I don't think so,' he replied, still looking at Kerry.

'Take a hint, dick,' she said.

The man turned to look at her. 'If I was talking to the shrivelled old boot, I'd be looking right at you.'

He felt a hand on his shoulder. Travis was standing behind the man.

'There's plenty more where he came from,' Kerry said.

Four of Michael Molloy's men came across. 'We're here to escort you out, sir.'

'What? I've only had a few drinks.'

'Now,' Greg Sampson said as Travis tightened his grip on the man.

'Alright, alright, I'm going. I only came here for the free drink. I didn't really want to talk to the ice maiden anyway.'

The men escorted Stuart out as Michael Molloy came across. 'Jesus, I'm sorry about that, ladies. I heard what he said, and I apologise, Rose. You too, Kerry. He's with one of the councillors. A lowlife hanger-on who thinks he walks on water. He's lucky he can walk out of here.'

Rose smiled. 'Michael, thank you for stepping in. And no need for the apology. We're having a good time.'

'Yes, don't worry about it, Michael. My man had it under control. But the backup is appreciated.'

'How are you ladies enjoying the evening so far?'

'I'm excited to see the model. This is going to be a very profitable venture for whoever wins,' Kerry said, giving Michael a little grin.

'Oh, it is indeed. Your unveiling was fantastic. I don't know how we're going to beat it.'

'You can but try.'

'Perhaps you would join me in a drink afterwards?'

'I'd love to, but I haven't seen your new hotel on the North Bridge. It would be nice to have a drink there.'

'Technically, it's my father's. I just help run the place.'

'Does he still have his floating restaurant?' Rose asked.

'Yes, he does, but when he gets somewhere new, it's like giving him a new toy.' He looked over and waved at a man. A man wearing a bowler hat, walking with a cane, and accompanied by an attractive woman.

'Adrian! Glad you could make it,' Michael said.

'I wouldn't miss it for the world. Considering the stake I have in it.' He smiled at Kerry and held out his hand while Fiona stood off to one side.

Kerry shook hands with him and Fiona.

'Good to see you again,' Fiona said. 'Hello, Rose.'

'Hi.'

'I don't see George Stone anywhere,' Jackson said to Michael.

'I had a feeling he wouldn't show.'

'Why don't us ladies go and get a drink?' Kerry said.

'Sounds good to me. I could murder a gin,' Fiona replied.

'Then let's go and murder one.'

TWENTY-SIX

'Right, get that fucking padlock off,' George Stone said from the passenger seat of the Range Rover. Being on Edinburgh City Council's planning committee, James Merchant wasn't used to being spoken to like this. He looked over at Stone from the driver's seat.

'Listen, I'm not sure about this.'

'Too late now. The time for uncertainty was before I offered you money, before you were sunning yourself on a yacht in the Mediterranean, before you were spending a luxury weekend in New York with a hooker. That was the time. That was then, this is now, and now means getting your arse out of that seat and getting that fucking padlock cut off and the gate open. The bolt cutters are behind you.'

'Fuck's sake,' Merchant said, getting out and

opening the back door. 'You might have brought one of your flunkies to do the job.'

'My flunkies don't get a two-grand escort hanging onto their arm. Hurry up before any daft bastard sees us.'

'We could have just walked along the roadway.'

'Do I look like a man who exercises? If I want to get out of breath, I'll—'

'I know, I know, you'll be on top of a two-grand hooker.'

'I was going to say, I'll join a gym, but trust you to think that way, manky bastard.'

Merchant slammed the back door a little too hard.

'Fucking brand-new motor, this is. And it's a fucking lease,' Stone said out loud as he watched Merchant walk towards the metal gate barring their way. 'Slam the fucking door.'

Merchant cut the padlock, opened the gate, walked back to the car, and got in behind the wheel, holding the bolt cutters out for Stone to take.

'Put them in the back. Do I look like I want my good clothes all fucking manky? Jesus, you're in a right strop tonight, Jimmy. Do you need more of those pills I gave you? Maybe if you'd taken one of the blue ones, you could have battered the gate down with your nob – save using the cutters.'

'I'm fine, thank you.' Merchant put the car in gear

and started driving. He stopped to close the gate then got back in.

'Don't go in a huff like a wee lassie. And put the fucking headlights out before one of those daft bastards from the stable block sees us.'

Merchant shook his head and turned the headlights off. It wasn't full dark, but dusk out in Penicuik, out in the woods, meant it was just as good as.

'Drive down to the bottom here and park at the side. Nobody else will be coming down.'

'Are you sure about this place?' Merchant asked. 'I mean, I know commuters are coming further and further out of town, but this seems to be a stretch.'

'Jimmy, as much as I admire your concern, everything will be fine. I will rebuild the old house first, then we'll start putting houses on the land. As soon as those ponces see the word *exclusive*, they'll be falling over themselves to put down a deposit.'

'I hope you're right, George.'

'Have you ever known me to be wrong? Just take a look at the apartment you're renting from me. They didn't appear by magic.'

'You're right. I shouldn't doubt you.'

At the intersection where the roads converged, Merchant stopped. 'What now?'

'Just park over to one side. We can't drive too close, but we can walk in the dark.'

'There are lights on outside the old stable block.'

'We're going a different way. Come on.' Stone got out of the big SUV, and Merchant gave him the key fob and followed. They walked along the road for a moment, then Stone pointed to a gate.

'We're going down here. We'll cut across the grass and then get up near the old house.'

'Christ, I hope you know what you're doing.'

'Of course I do. I want you to see this place. You were interested in all the others because I was giving you a bung. You're getting the same deal here too, Jimmy. When you see the place for yourself, you'll have no problem being on board.' *Or I might just have to send some half-wit round for a chat, somebody who couldn't find his own arsehole if he stuck a firework up it, but who could rip your legs from their sockets.*

'I can see the attraction out here, to be honest. The peace and tranquillity,' Merchant said.

'I knew you would see it my way.' They walked down what amounted to a ramp covered in grass. A wall was on their right, with a ditch in front of it, grass coming right up to its edge. It was a ha-ha.

It was almost full dark now, the stars above looking down on the two men walking over the grass field. They kept close to the wall, and when they got near the ruins of Preston House, they climbed back out again.

What was once a grand Palladian mansion, was now merely a shell.

'When was the last time you were here?' George Stone said.

'I've never been here before.'

'Really? They had to have planning permission to stick a café on the side of it.'

'I sent one of the underlings to inspect it and do any necessary paperwork. I didn't think the great George Stone would one day be interested in it. I mean, it isn't officially for sale.'

'Not yet, Jimmy, not yet,' Stone said. 'But I'll soon make sure it's for sale.'

'How in God's name are you going to do that?'

'It's still a private concern, isn't it?'

'Yes, but the family who own it open it up to the public in the summer. Hence the café.'

'Money talks my friend. I'll make them an offer they can't refuse.'

'What if they do refuse?'

'There are ways and means.'

'Jesus.'

They walked through the dark to the back of the house.

'Where are we going?' Merchant asked.

'Down here.'

There was a grass ramp that led up to what was

once a back entrance into the mansion. Merchant looked at the building in the dark, at the windows where glass had once been, at a bricked-up doorway where once people had walked through.

But it was a doorway underneath the ramp that Stone was interested in.

'What's in there?' Merchant said, keeping his voice low.

'You'll see.' They went down a set of steps until they reached the doorway. It was dark inside, so they took out a little LED torch and shone them about. The light picked out a stone corridor, that turned left. It continued along until it turned right. A doorway was at the end. Merchant saw the stone staircase.

'Where does that lead to?'

'It's an old cellar.' Stone shone his torch around.

'What are we doing here?' Merchant asked.

'You were an architect, weren't you?'

'You know I was.'

'I've brought you here in confidence, Jimmy. I want you to run your eyes over this place and see what you think.'

'I think that there was something down here at one time, before the stones were put in place. But whoever did this, they were clever. You can't see the joins. Unless it was just a staircase that leads to nowhere.'

'If it did lead somewhere, would you be able to get through here?'

'Yes, it could be done.'

'Good. That's what I wanted to hear, because...' Stone reached out and pushed a part of the wall and it swung slowly open to reveal a doorway.

'What the hell?' Merchant said. 'How did you know that was there?'

'Never mind that. I want you to have a look and see how stable you think this place is. I want us to go down there.'

'Okay.'

They went down three levels of stairs until they came into a hexagonal room, with a doorway in each wall, including the one they'd come down. Their flashlights cut through the darkness, revealing a pattern in the floor.

'You seen anything like that before?' Stone asked.

'No, nothing.'

'There are more like this down each corridor. Let me show you this one down here.'

'Wait, George.'

'What's wrong?'

'I need a piss.'

'For fuck's sake. Can you not hold it in?'

'I'm touching cloth.'

'You could have had a pish in the bushes outside.

Why did you wait until we came in here?' Stone shook his head and made a face.

'I didn't need to go out there. It's the cold in here. The cold affects my bladder.'

'Having those wine spritzers you guzzle affects your bladder.'

'I only had two. Since I was driving.'

'Bloody wine spritzer. My wife drinks those but she's a woman. You're not trying to tell me something are you?'

'Of course not. I just like wine. There's a name for people who appreciate wine.'

'Winos.'

'Connoisseurs.'

'I think winos pish themselves more than connoisseurs do. Go down one of those corridors. And use the hand sanitiser I keep in the car when we get back and do not, and I repeat, *do not* try and shake my hand when we part tonight. Now fuck off down there.'

'There's just one problem.'

'What now? You don't want to splash your good Oxfords?'

'No. I have shy bladder.'

'What's that?'

'You know... I can't go when there's anybody else around.'

'You can't have a pish in front of anybody?'

'Exactly.'

'You wouldn't have lasted five minutes in the army,' Stone said. 'Hurry up for fuck's sake. That's all we need, for somebody to come in here and see you with your skids round your ankles.'

'Thanks, George, I get the idea.' Merchant walked along a corridor, then his light disappeared.

'You're not listening, are you George?' Merchant said, his voice bouncing off the stone walls.

'Believe it or not, that is not a pastime of mine. Listening to a wino having a pish.' He walked along another corridor, feeling the air icy. He shone the light around, but the walls here looked just like the others.

After a few minutes, he walked back along to the hexagonal room in the middle. 'Jimmy? You finished yet, or do you want me to start whistling or something?'

Silence.

'Jimmy?' Nothing. 'Jimmy, I'm starting to think I should make a Facebook post about you tampering with yourself. Are you finished or not?'

Still silence.

'If this is your idea of a prank, you have to know I don't like practical jokes.'

Still silence.

'For fuck's sake, Jimmy. You're going to be off my Christmas card list at this rate.' Starting to think Merchant had maybe had a heart attack or something,

Stone walked down the corridor that the other man had gone down.

'I'm coming along, so if you still have your wee man out, you'd better tell me. Jimmy?' Stone's light reached the end of the corridor and hit the wall. Merchant wasn't there. Stone thought he had gone in the wrong passageway, so he went into the one next to it. That too was empty. As were the others.

'Christ, don't tell me you went outside.' Stone went up the steps until he reached the corridor that led outside.

Merchant was nowhere to be seen.

Had he bottled out and gone back to the car? Stone started making his way back. If he saw Merchant standing next to some bushes, he'd make sure the man would be sitting down for a piss for a long time to come.

Merchant wasn't at the car either. Angry and thinking the man had bottled out and left, Stone got into the Range Rover and started driving away.

TWENTY-SEVEN

'How did you get on, son?' Andy Watt said to Bruce Hagan. They were in a side room in the hotel. Lou was in the main crowd with his friend Larry.

'Andy, she left Langholm a few weeks ago. We spoke to a friend of hers down there, and a pathologist that Ross was with friends with hanged himself. You might have to be the one to make a phone call down to Dumfries to see if there were any suspicious circumstances.'

'Jesus! I can do that.'

'Do you know where she's staying?'

'No, Bruce. And there are so many hotels and service apartments it would be impossible to find her. She might even have rented a flat for all I know.'

Hagan was quiet for a few seconds. 'You don't

think she had anything to do with Jean's attack, do you?'

'You know what we say about coincidences, mate. And I'm pissed off that they won't even let me go to see Jean.'

'You said the daughter was a bitch.'

'She is. A real shit-stirrer.'

'Maybe she's just having a hard time after what happened to her father.'

Watt looked at him. 'What do you mean?'

'I hope you don't mind, but we had a quiet spell so I did some digging. You didn't know that her father died?'

'Yes, of course I did.'

'Did you know he was stabbed to death after he got into a fight with somebody?'

'Christ, no I didn't.'

'Here's another phone call for you to make; call the Met and see what they have on him. I did an online search and his name came up a few times on him being arrested. Once for battering somebody with a baseball bat, which he claimed was self-defence. He said he took it from his attacker and hit him with it. Several times for drug possession. He was a bad bastard, looks like.'

Watt patted him on the arm. 'Thanks for that. I owe you one.'

'Anytime. Now I've got to go and mingle. Me, Lou, and Larry are here keeping an eye on a suspected cheating husband but finding out about that louse from London was getting my juices flowing, let me tell you.'

'I'll bet. You were a good copper, son.'

'It is what it is though. I can't turn back the clock. This is the closest thing to it, and Lou is a great help. I'm going to ask Larry if he wants to come on board too. I mean, who would suspect two old blokes are following them?'

'Good point.'

They went back through to the ballroom. Miller and Purcell were there, dressed smartly but not in the suits that made them look like policemen wherever they went. Jeni Bridge was with them, dressed smart but casual.

A huge table was set at the far end of the ballroom, covered in a sheet. Beautiful women in black dresses, who probably stood next to cars at car shows, stood ready to pull the sheet off. A five-piece band was playing in the background.

Robert Molloy was on the stage with his son Michael.

'I'm surprised Molloy hasn't snagged himself a wife by now,' Miller said to Purcell.

'Would you want to live with him?'

'I'm sure somebody would. By the way, did you see

Lou?'

'A one-man Tartan Day parade.'

'He looks very dapper,' Jeni said.

'I know he does, I just don't want to tell the old sod that.'

Paddy Gibb came across to stand next to them. 'Steffi Walker, Julie Stott, and Hazel are sitting talking, but they're filming with their mobile phones, making it look like they're snapping chat or something.'

'Good God, Paddy, even I know it's Snapchat and I'm an old fart,' Jeni Bridge said.

Molloy started speaking and everybody who knew his reputation stopped talking immediately. The voices were silent, the band stopped playing and Molloy continued.

'Ladies and gentlemen, welcome to the unveiling of our design for the New Town North Project. I won't give a long, boring, drawn out speech, so without further ado, ladies, will you please do the honours?'

The models pulled the sheet back to reveal a huge 3D model of what the new project would look like if they got the go-ahead.

Robert Molloy came off the stage with Michael, and they shook some hands before making their way to the back of the room where Kerry Hamilton was standing. Tables were set around the periphery, with an army of servers waiting to seat the guests so dinner could be served.

'What do you think, Kerry?' Molloy said.

'It looks fantastic, Robert. I think it's going to win.'

'I think so, too. Despite his expertise, I don't think Stone will come up with a better design. And our plans are now in the hands of the committee so they can go through them with a fine-tooth comb. Once Stone has his unveiling, I think we'll be home and dry.'

'Agreed,' she said, taking a glass of champagne off a tray that was going round.

'I took the liberty of having you placed at my table.'

'Excellent. I'm seriously impressed.'

'I thought you would be,' Robert said, smiling at her.

TWENTY-EIGHT

Davy Dickson and Des Crawley were in the back of the transit van being driven by two blokes they had never met before.

'I hope they're not sex traffickers,' Crawley said.

'I think your arsehole is quite safe.'

'Next time you want to punch Jackson in the mouth, I won't stop you.'

'Shut up, for fuck's sake. They might be listening. And for the record, if you are listening, he's just talking shite.' Dickson shook his head. 'I'm telling you, if this job goes tits up, and they say one of us has to die, I'm going to tell them you said they were a pair of fannies.'

'I bet you would, ya bastard. But you know who those guys are, don't you?'

'Oh, let me see? Michael Ball and Bono.'

'They're ex-army.'

'They're a great couple of lads,' Dickson said, raising his voice slightly.

'They're not going to hear you through the metal.' Crawley shook his head.

A short distance later, the van stopped. They heard the front doors open then a few seconds later, the back doors opened.

All the men were dressed in black, but there were two tool bags in beside the security guards.

'Grab those bags, lads. And remember, if anybody asks, we're here to fix something,' the taller man said, obviously the boss. He had a long, black tube slung over one shoulder.

'You got it,' Dickson said, trying to sound tough.

They stood in Moray Place, in the West End. One of the townhouses had scaffolding up it, covered in green netting.

'We're going in there. Follow me.'

Dickson and Crawley followed him while the other guy closed the van doors. They walked up the stone steps until they came to the front door. It was a make-shift steel entrance door, put in place for security reasons. The leader took out a key and undid the padlock. The door swung outwards and then the glass-paned inner door was unlocked and in they went, the second man pulling the steel door closed while the inner one stayed open.

They took out torches and shone them on the stairs.

'Where are we going?' Crawley asked.

'Just follow him,' the second man said, bringing up the rear. From the ground floor, they went up three levels, each one looking like a building site, until they got to the top. The leader stopped at what they thought was a closet, but when he opened it, more stairs led up to a small landing. A ladder led to a hatch in the roof. The leader stepped up two rungs, reached up, and pushed the hatch. It swung up on hinges, and he kept hold of it, lowering it as he climbed higher.

'I told you they would hear us,' Crawley whispered. 'Now they're going to throw us off the roof.'

'Oh don't talk pish. Hurry up and get up there.'

He watched as his friend climbed up onto the roof, before making the climb himself. It was windy up here, and dark. Davy Dickson felt more scared than he had felt in a very long time.

'Keep low,' the leader said. 'We're going over the dividing wall, across the other roof, and over the next dividing wall where we will be going into the building via the hatch just like this one. Got that?'

Both guards nodded. The leader started walking in a crouch while the second man lowered their hatch.

'This is exciting, isn't it?' Crawley said.

'A minute ago, you were pishing your pants. Now you're on an SAS mission, you've got a hard-on.'

'Hey, this is something we can brag to lassies about.'

'No, it's not. Bragging about breaking into a house? Not unless you want to spend time in Saughton.'

'Hurry up you two,' the second guy said. 'Pair of sweetie wives.'

Crawley made a face at Dickson before they ducked and ran, following the leader through the darkness as the man made his way over the wall. It was only a couple of feet high and they got over easily. The wind made Dickson feel uneasy but this spurred him on and once they were over the next wall, they saw the leader stopped at another hatch just like the one they had come up through.

'This is a fire egress point, so it's not locked,' he said. He squeezed a handle and the hatch lifted. He shone his torch down, located the ladder, and stepped over and down. They all followed and went down the stairs to the door and out onto a landing.

This house was offices, not an empty shell that was being refurbished. They made it to the first floor.

'How do you guys know where to go?' Crawley asked.

'Never mind that.' He took the black tube off and held it in one hand. 'You two go downstairs and keep an eye open. That's all you have to do. Nothing more, nothing less.'

They went downstairs, leaving the ex-soldiers to do whatever it was they did.

'I thought you said we could help ourselves to stuff?' Crawley said.

'I thought we were going into a house. With jewellery and stuff. There's not even a TV we can chorey.'

'Everybody has a big flat screen nowadays. We could hardly take it up on the roof.'

'No, but we could grab a few things and then nip out the front door and stick it in the van.'

'And get a kicking for our troubles? No thanks. Besides, Jackson said he will be paying us a bonus. And he didn't fire us. Win win, my friend.'

Before Crawley could steal a fax machine, the second in command came down for them. 'Let's go.'

'Can we not just leave through the front door?' Crawley said.

'That's not how we work, pal. Nobody must know we were here.'

Crawley shrugged and they went back up the way they had come.

Ten minutes later, they were back in the van. Without a TV.

TWENTY-NINE

'*Well, would you look at that,*' Angel said, as they sat in the little rented car in the parking spaces opposite the church in Bellevue Crescent.

Maggie Parks came up the steps and walked over to her car, got in, and drove away.

'He didn't wait long, did he?' Eve whispered. Her heart was beating so hard she thought it was going to explode.

'*He certainly did not. He told you he was divorced and he slept with you, leading you on. You find out he was living in a house with that other woman—*'

Eve held up a hand. 'Stop. He said he had been in a relationship but they slept in separate rooms. Living separate lives.'

'*So what's his excuse now? He moves out of that big house and into this one with this woman.*'

'It could be his sister.' Eve looked at her, tears in her eyes.

'I'm not even going to dignify that with an answer.' Angel looked at her in the darkness. *'Why don't you go in and have a look around?'*

'I don't know how to break into a house.'

'You have the lock-pick kit, don't you?'

'Yes.'

'Then I'll teach you right now. It's easy.'

They got out of the car and walked across to Paddy Gibb's flat, going quickly down the steps. Eve took the kit out of her pocket and took the picks out. With Angel's guidance, she had the door open in under a minute.

She opened the door and stood listening for any sounds that somebody was home. Nothing. No TV. A weak light was coming from around a door. She gently closed the front door behind them and walked along the hallway to an open door. It was the living room. She was prepared to fight if she had to, but nobody was in the room. She opened another door. A bedroom. Andy's room, she thought when she saw the suitcase over by the wardrobe door.

Her insides tumbled when she opened a drawer and ran her hand through his things. She took clothing out, his underwear and socks. Then some T-shirts.

'How can he do this to me?' Eve said. 'He moves in

here but has a girlfriend coming in? Didn't he get my letters?'

'Of course he did. You thought he was waiting for you and all this time, he was leading you on. The bastard!' Angel started pacing, a sure sign that she was getting angrier. *'I want to burn this place down!'*

'Easy, Angel. I haven't even seen him since I came to Edinburgh.'

'Well, do something about it, Eve! Go and talk to him. Have it out with him.'

Eve carried on raking about, getting angrier by the minute. But she knew that if she trashed the place, then he would know she had been in here. So she started tidying up, putting the clothes back so it looked the way it had looked when she came in. This was the way she would get Andy to see he should be with her, and not that bitch.

'Let's get out of here, Angel. I'll meet Andy, pretend I don't know why he hasn't written back to me.'

'You still want to be with him?'

'Of course I do. It's why Simon and I had to part ways. I want to be with Andy more than anything and I will do whatever it takes to achieve that.'

Eve and Angel walked out of the front door and gently closed it behind them.

THIRTY

'That went very well, I think,' Robert Molloy said in his office in the hotel on North Bridge.

Kerry Hamilton and Rose, Adrian and Fiona Jackson, and Michael Molloy were holding up glasses of champagne.

'Here's to us,' Jackson said. 'I just wish George Stone had turned up to see how well it went.'

'He'll be crying into his soup when he finds out that he lost. And he will lose,' Kerry said.

Rose looked confused. 'I'm not sure what we're doing here,' she whispered to Kerry.

Kerry smiled and put an arm round the woman's shoulders. 'Let me just say, this is one time George Stone isn't going to get his own way.'

'Please don't be offended,' Robert said to Kerry,

'but this is a delicate matter. How much do you trust Rose here?'

Rose turned to Molloy, a sudden anger on her face. 'Trust me? Let me tell you something; I've seen that girl at her best, and I've seen her at her worst. I've known her for over twenty years. I've seen her laughing at a birthday party, and I've seen her lying in a public toilet, almost dying. I love her like she's my own flesh and blood and I would give my life for her, so don't you ever ask her how much she can trust me!' Her voice was rising now and there were tears in her eyes.

Molloy smiled and raised a glass to her. 'Kerry, you did tell me she was passionate about you, and I can see that. You passed the test, Rose. Now have another glass of champagne. You're on board.'

Rose looked confused for a moment.

Molloy topped up her glass. 'In our business, trust is everything.' He clinked her glass as Kerry put an arm round her shoulders.

'I love you, Rose,' she said.

'I love you, too.'

'I know Robert is going to win the competition. But let me ask you this; how can you be so sure when George Stone still has to unveil his project?' Fiona asked her husband.

Adrian Jackson smiled. 'Tonight, I had a couple of my men enter Stone's office and swap out the plans for

Stone's bid with slightly altered ones. They were done by a master forger, and they are identical. Almost. There are just some subtle changes, which will get them knocked back from the council when they go over them again. They have to be submitted at the time of the unveiling. We submitted ours tonight.'

'Won't Stone notice?' Fiona said.

'Of course he will. But he'll think Dempsey screwed up. Or one of his team. They'll be running about like headless chickens.'

She looked at her husband. 'No secrets you said.'

'This is why we're telling you now. I wanted to make sure everything went smoothly.'

'Fair enough. But what I find strange is why Miss Hamilton is here.'

Kerry smiled at her. 'Robert and my father go back a long way. We thought it was better to team up. My submission was just a smokescreen. It failed because it was garbage. I am part of Robert and Michael's consortium. In fact, myself, Adrian, and the Molloys are the consortium. I am backing Robert's bid as it is my bid as well. There are no laws about me being in his consortium, as long as his name is on the bid. Stone is a prick who needs taking down a peg or two. You know the university at Craiglockhart where he's building houses? That was something Robert was interested in buying. As soon as Stone found out, he had his flunky in the council do his magic so Stone's permits were granted. Robert's weren't. Stone doesn't play by the rules, so neither do we.'

'I wonder why Stone didn't turn up tonight?' Jackson said, looking at Robert.

'He was probably admitting defeat and felt embarrassed about it.'

'Don't underestimate him,' said Michael.

THIRTY-ONE

'The middle of June and it hasn't rained in days,' Watt said as he got out of the car. 'I think aliens are playing about with our weather.'

'The same ones who made the earth flat?' Gibb said from the back seat as Miller killed the engine.

'Don't you knock it, Paddy. We don't know what's out there. You know how secretive NASA are. The aliens are probably in parliament by now. I mean, who else would let their country be run by a bunch of gin-sodden old fannies?'

'Just try and concentrate on why we're out here in the middle of nowhere,' Gibb said, taking out his cigarettes. 'They haven't banned smoking out in the countryside, have they?'

'Give them time,' Miller said.

'I'm glad the likes of Paddy smoke. We'd be paying ten quid for a gallon of milk otherwise. All those old windbags know is how to tax us.'

'Remember that the next time I light up in the car,' Paddy said, blowing smoke out into the air.

The mortuary van was sitting waiting in line with the other emergency vehicles. A uniform was talking to a tall, older man.

'I hope Jake Dagger got woken up out of his scratcher. I wonder how many Saturdays he has to work?' Watt said.

'Death never takes a break,' Miller said.

'Agreed. But you know Dagger; he likes to get pished on a Friday night.'

Gibb walked over to the man, nipping his cigarette and putting it back in the pack. *You're dead later on, you little bastard.*

'This is the gentleman who called it in, sir,' he said. 'Jack Harris.'

Harris turned to look at the detectives. The ruins of Preston House would have looked magnificent as a backdrop had it not been for all the emergency vehicles. A specialist fire service truck was off to one side, along with an aerial rescue truck.

'Thanks. We'll take it from here.'

The uniform nodded and walked away.

Gibb introduced his team to Harris. 'Tell me how you found the body,' he said, turning to look at the scaffolding that was holding the interior of the ruin together. Men were up there and sheets had been positioned to block the view from people below.

'I walk my dog here.'

Watt looked at the man's feet and didn't see an animal.

'Well, he's back in the car now, of course.'

'You were out walking your dog,' Miller said, 'then what?'

'Jasper started whimpering and I wondered if there was somebody creeping about. We had problems with junkies a while back, but the police started doing extra patrols in here and I think that helped stop them coming back. But Jasper kept on whimpering, and I looked up at the scaffolding around the house and there it was; a body. I called 999.'

'Apart from junkies, did you ever see strangers hanging about?'

'There are plenty of strangers, but they're mostly dog walkers like me or people exercising. This place is open to the public.'

'Okay, sir, thank you for that,' Gibb said. 'We'll need a formal statement down at the station, but you can pop into the local one and they'll send it to us.'

Harris walked away.

They watched as the aerial rescue truck lowered its boom to the ground and one of the pathologists, Jake Dagger, stepped out.

'I always said you were for higher things, Dagger,' Watt said.

'Bloody heights,' Dagger said 'What is wrong with people these days? Putting a body up there.'

'They did it just to piss you off,' Watt said.

'Still bumming a room off Paddy, I take it?' Dagger said.

'Only until you've got your spare room sorted.'

'I don't have one.'

'Dagger, tell us what was going on up there before my bloody head explodes. I'm not used to getting up early on a Saturday morning,' Gibb said.

'It's ten o'clock, Paddy,' Miller said.

'Now it is. It wasn't when my bloody phone went. And he was snoring like a bloody pig,' he said, nodding to Watt. The three men looked at him. 'I could hear him in the other room, for God's sake.'

'Besides, he has a girlfriend,' Watt said, realising his mistake after the words left his mouth. 'Manky Mary from Musselburgh. She works on the chat lines.'

'Anyway,' Dagger continued, 'he's been impaled on a crude, home-made spear.'

'Any ID on him?'

'Yes. I went through his pockets and got a wallet. His name's James Merchant. Works for Edinburgh Council planning department.'

'How do you know that?'

'I've met him before. I work for the council too, remember?'

'Right, once the ID branch have been all over him, get him down. I'll have his next of kin told and we'll make arrangements for a formal ID.'

Jack Harris came across to the detectives. 'I just remembered,' he said, 'when I was taking Jasper back to the car, I saw a strange car parked along the road there.'

They turned to look in the direction where Harris was pointing.

'I went and had a look. It was a Range Rover. That's the number plate.' He handed a piece of paper to Gibb.

'Thank you.' He handed the paper to Watt. 'Go and speak to somebody about this.'

Watt took it and walked away from the others to get on his phone and contact control in Bilston for a PNC check.

Five minutes later, he was back. 'It's registered to a van.'

'You sure?' Gibb said.

'That's what I was told.'

'Somebody didn't want to be identified. Obviously, Merchant's killer,' Gibb said.

'Unless Range Rover have started making tractors these days.'

THIRTY-TWO

Miller was finishing up at the station while Gibb and Watt went to break the news to James Merchant's wife, now widow. He was walking along the corridor when he saw Jeni Bridge approaching.

'Shouldn't you be at home with your little girls?' she said. Her face looked tired, her eyes red, like she'd been drinking. 'I know, I look a mess. I wasn't drunk last night, but I'm having problems with my daughter, that's all. And trust me, Frank Miller, you'll cry more than once when they're growing up.'

'Kim has the girls at her mum's.' Miller was quiet for a moment, wondering if he should mention seeing her daughter, but if the problem was big enough to make her cry so hard she looked like she was on drugs, then maybe it was for the best if he did.

'Listen, ma'am, this might be none of my business, but I saw a woman who looks extremely like your daughter. I remembered seeing the photo in your office.'

'You did? Where?' There was an edge of desperation in her voice.

'Before I say, can I look at the photo again. I'd hate to make a fuss if I was wrong.'

'Step this way.'

In her office, she picked up the framed photo and showed it to him.

'That's her,' he said.

Jeni put the photo back down. 'Tell me where you saw her. I thought she went back to Glasgow with her boyfriend.'

'We're investigating the mugging of Andy Watt's girlfriend, Jean Melrose. When we went to talk to her daughter, your daughter was in the house. She introduced herself as Lynn Rogers, but I thought I recognised her.'

'Rogers is my maiden name. Christ, I need to see her. Come with me, will you Frank?'

'Of course I will.'

They made their way down to the rear car park, stopping to pick up the keys to a pool car on the way.

'Paddy, I want to show you something. In my room,' Andy Watt said. He and Gibb had just got home after giving the death message to James Merchant's widow.

'Look, son, I know you split with your girlfriend, but you'll find somebody else. You don't need me in your room.'

'Don't flatter yourself.'

Gibb put down his sandwich and followed Watt into the room. 'What is it?'

'At least try to feign interest.'

'You interrupted my ham sandwich, so it better be good.'

'I think somebody's been in here. In my room.'

'You're not accusing Maggie of being a tea leaf I hope.'

'No, no, nothing like that. It's just a feeling, like the one I had in Langholm when I thought that nosy old boot of a landlady had been going through my skids drawer. I never gave it any thought because nothing was missing.'

'Is there something missing from here?'

'No. But I am fussy about where my stuff goes, and although I haven't a lot here, everything goes into a drawer the same way, so no matter where I am, the top drawer has my skids and socks, skids on the left, socks on the right.'

'So what's wrong?'

Watt pulled open the top drawer of the chest of drawers where his clothes were. Gibb looked in.

'Socks on the left and underwear on the right, in exactly the opposite position to where they were before.'

'Didn't you notice when you were getting dressed this morning?'

'I was in so much of a hurry, I didn't notice, but something seemed odd, and then we were in a rush to get to the murder scene. It was just now that it clicked. I think Eve Ross has been in here.'

A few minutes later, Maggie came in. 'Don't let me disturb you. You seem like you're having fun.'

'Hello, sweetheart,' Gibb said.

'What are you boys up to? You look like you're plotting the perfect crime.'

'No, but I think we're part of one,' Watt said.

Maggie looked puzzled. 'What's wrong?'

'Don't laugh,' Gibb said, 'but Andy's Y-fronts are in the wrong place in the drawer.'

Maggie smirked. 'Okay.'

'Seriously, love. Andy thinks somebody let themselves in and rummaged about but put things back to cover their tracks, except they made a mistake.'

Now Maggie wasn't smiling. 'Are you sure about this, Andy?'

'I am, Maggie.'

She left the room and they heard her moving stuff. She came back with what looked like an old tool case. 'We have new equipment, and like a hoarder, I couldn't bear to get rid of this one, so I kept it.'

She asked them to leave then got to work, dusting for prints. A little while later, the dust was down and she started lifting prints, especially on the chest of drawers. 'I can have these run through the system, as a matter of priority. I want to know if somebody else really was in here.'

'What if there are multiple prints on here?' Watt said.

'I bought this unit a few weeks ago in Ikea. Paddy and I assembled it and it's been cleaned multiple times. The only prints on there should be us three. We'll know by this afternoon. And if I think this was a ploy to get rid of me while you both watch football on TV, a soccer ball will not be the only thing getting kicked.'

Miller made good time, with the lights and sirens on the unmarked car. He pulled up in front of Jean Melrose's house, having switched the siren off up at the main road.

Jeni had the door open before the engine was even

switched off. By the time Miller caught up with her, Jeni was through the gates and banging on Jean's front door.

A man answered. Mark, Miller remembered. He didn't look high this time. He looked scared.

'What is it?' he said, wrapping his arms around himself.

'I want to see my daughter,' Jeni said.

'Who are you?'

'I'm her mother,' she said, about to step into the house.

'Whoa, whoa,' Mark said, putting a hand out. 'You got a warrant?'

'No.'

'Then you can't come in.'

'Are you the young man who picked her up?'

'Listen, lady. Lynn was here, but she left. We had a fight and she left. Where to, I don't know.'

'She wouldn't just leave.'

'What can I tell you, missus. Your daughter left.'

'When? How long ago?'

'Yesterday sometime. I don't know exactly.'

'I want to speak to Jean's daughter.'

'She's not here. She went out. I don't know when she'll be back.'

Mark stepped back and slammed the door shut.

Jeni gritted her teeth. 'Bastard. I'm going to kick that door in.' She took a step back and Miller grabbed hold of her arm.

'Ma'am, that isn't going to help.'

She pulled her arm away. 'You should have fucking told me about this before now.'

Miller stayed silent.

'Christ, I'm sorry, Frank. If it wasn't for you, I wouldn't even know she'd been here. And I don't believe for one second that she just left. If anything, she would have come home to me.'

'Do you think she could have gone through to her father in Glasgow?'

'I'll find out right now.' Jeni took out her phone and dialled a number and spoke to her ex-husband before hanging up. 'No, she's not there.'

'I hate to be the voice of reason, but there's not much else we can do. No crime's been committed.'

'I know, and that's the bastard of it all. But that piece of shit is lying, I just know it.'

'I think so too.'

Lynn Bridge had wet herself. She had tried not to, but the man's hand on her face felt rough, and the knife he was holding in his other hand looked like it could cut a horse in two.

'Where's the money? I want you to think about it carefully and talk to me in a civilised manner, and maybe I won't start slicing you. Do you understand?'

His cockney accent was strong, so strong that sometimes she couldn't understand him. She understood him this time though. He took his hand away.

'I don't know what you're talking about.'

'I had a feeling you were going to say that.' He slapped her so hard, she fell sideways, the chair she was tied to crashing against the floor.

They heard banging on the front door.

'If your boyfriend says anything to anybody, I'll slit your throat, you know that, right?'

Lynn nodded.

'Jesus, you don't 'arf smell of piss. I'm glad you're not my fucking girlfriend.'

A few minutes later, Mark came into the room followed by his captor.

'He did very well,' the captor said. 'It was her mother. Mark got rid of her.'

'Good boy, Mark. Now you can have another little think and tell us where Abi put the money she stole.'

'She didn't tell me anything about money, I swear.'

'Oh, he swears,' the leader said. Then he looked at Mark. 'I don't believe you.'

'You want me to tie him up again?' the second one said.

'Oh yes. Now we go to the second phase. Where we cause real pain.'

THIRTY-THREE

'They're going to find out it's not me,' James Merchant said, pacing up and down George Stone's living room.

Stone laughed. 'Fucking lucky I put those tractor plates on the car.'

Merchant stopped and poured himself another whisky. 'Thank Christ you seen me running at the last minute or that old bastard would have had his fucking pals all over me.'

'Well, to give him his due, you *were* standing in that basement with your willie in your hand.'

'You can laugh, George, but luckily I watched some You Tube videos on how to get out of a choke hold. How to stop a street fight with one punch, stuff like that.'

'Obviously, you watched one on how to run like fuck when there's a gang of weirdos chasing you.'

'With fucking spears no less. I nearly shat myself.'

'Tell me again what happened.'

'I told you last night,' Merchant said.

'Jimmy, I was trying to get us away from those nutters.'

Merchant sat down. 'I was about to have a pish in one of those passageways when all of a sudden I sense somebody behind me. I thought it was you, coming to wind me up. Then when I was about to turn round, I felt an arm go around my neck. I was being put into a choke hold. The thing is, there was another corridor off that one, like there was a doorway. I was dragged into it and the doorway closed.

'But that was when I fought back. Not out of any sense of being a hard man, but fear. I didn't know who this was, or where he was trying to take me. I felt a hand go into my pocket and take my wallet. That was his mistake. His grip loosened and I made a move, grabbing his arm and twisting it.'

'And you didn't get your wallet back.'

'I was looking, but he had taken my flashlight. He had it but he dropped it when I started fighting him. It was rolling about on the floor but I didn't see my wallet. I thought I was stuck in there but I pushed against the wall and it opened again. When I got back to the middle, you were gone.'

'I was looking for you.'

'I know you were. But I thought you would go back to the car if you couldn't find me, thinking that *I* had gone back to the car, even though you had the keys. And then when I was running along that road, I turned and saw those arseholes chasing me. And you know the rest.'

'They killed the man, the one I assume you were fighting. He failed and they made him pay with his life,' Stone said.

'They know where I live now. I was going to go home but the police would already have been there telling my wife.'

'I bet she's been on to the insurance company by now.'

'Wouldn't surprise me. Probably shagging the milkman as well.'

'Seriously though, those fuckers might go to your house. Just as well they don't know about the apartment I let you use as a shagging pad. You could always crash there. Tell your wife a mate left town and asked you to look after it. None of the bills are in your name.'

'I could. Thanks, George.'

'That's what friends are for. But you are going to have to tell her you're still alive first. The police will wonder how the dead guy got your wallet. You could tell them you were out drinking with a friend last night, and lost your wallet. Your friend paid for the taxi and you crashed at his place.'

'Good idea.'

'And we're going to have to watch our backs. I'll get some men to drive us about. But I can't help wondering; why put a spear through that bloke and leave him up on the scaffolding?'

'That's easy, George. They knew it would be on TV so you would see it. They were sending a message to you. This is not over.'

THIRTY-FOUR

Robert Molloy was shaking as he walked along the corridor to Jean Melrose's room in the Royal Infirmary. It smelled of polish and something faintly nauseating.

There was a uniformed officer guarding the door outside. He put up a hand when Molloy and his two men approached.

'Who are you?' the young officer said.

'I'm a friend of Ms Melrose. I'm here to see her.'

'It's only family allowed.'

'Look, sonny, get the fu—'

The door opened and Frank Miller looked out. 'It's okay. Go and have a coffee break.'

'Yes, sir.'

Molloy gritted his teeth as the young man walked away.

'Come in,' Miller said. 'And don't get upset with him, he's here to protect Jean.'

'Aye, you're right,' he said, coming into the room and closing the door behind him. Molloy looked at Jean, her body seemingly covered in wires. But she was awake.

'Christ Almighty, Jean. What did they do to you?' Molloy said, and there were tears rolling down his cheeks. 'Was this your daughter who did this?'

Jean blinked and very slowly shook her head. 'No. They're going to hurt her, Robert,' she answered, her voice a faint whisper.

'Who is? The men who attacked you?'

Very slowly, she nodded. 'They said they want their money back or we're both dead.'

'What money, Jean?' Molloy looked at Miller before looking back down at his friend.

'I don't know. They think we have their money. It was a woman, Robert. I think they've hurt Abi.'

Her breath started coming in rasps. 'Take it easy,' Miller said. 'I'll get a nurse to get you a drink.'

They stepped out into the corridor and Miller told a nurse that Jean needed attention. The uniform hadn't gone far and was standing with a coffee further along. Miller waved for him to come back.

'We're going now. Don't move from this spot.'

Molloy looked at his two men. 'You two stay here as backup. If anybody tries to get in there—'

'The uniform will deal with it,' Miller interrupted.

'Aye, he can deal with it.' An understanding look passed between the men, then Molloy walked away with Miller.

'How did you know to call me?' he said when they were walking alone.

'I saw a photo of you with Jean, taken discreetly. I knew then that she was one of your people. Then when we went to Jean's house, to talk to Abi, her junkie boyfriend said she left. I think he was lying. He went there with Jeni Bridge's daughter, and he's a friend of Abi's, but he said to Jeni that Abi had also left. I think they're being held there.'

'You don't think the Bridge girl and that ponce attacked Jean, do you?'

'No, I don't. This guy doesn't look like he has it in him.'

'What are you lot planning now?' Molloy said.

'Jeni Bridge and I were not allowed in the house, and since no crime has been committed in the residence, our hands are tied. I just wanted to make you aware of what was going on since Jean's a friend of yours.' He stopped and looked at Molloy. 'I understand Jean met up with Rick Dempsey. Was that your doing?'

'You know I can't talk business with you, but considering you called me, I'll give you this; Dempsey's best interests were for me, not George Stone. He just kept his eyes and ears open.'

'Is that what it was like for Andy Watt? You had Jean passing on information to you?'

'Believe it or not, she met that chimp online. He didn't tell her at first that he was a copper. When I found out, I admit I ran that idea past her, but she said no. And that's the truth. I've known Jean for a long time. I gave her the interior designer contracts for my new properties if she would liaise with Dempsey. Unscrupulous yes, but she was happy with Watt until he fucked around on her.'

'He's human. He made a mistake. It happens.'

'If that was anybody else... well, I'll leave you to fill in the blanks.'

'Consider them filled in.'

'Right,' Molloy said, 'what's this joker's name who wouldn't let you into Jean's house?'

'You know I can't give you that name. He won't let you in.'

'Yes, he fucking will. You see, Frank, I own that fucking house. Jean has lived in it rent free for years. And nobody will tell me I can't go into my own house, I can assure you.'

'There could be a gang in there. Mark... my words.'

Molloy nodded, understanding. *Mark*. 'I'd invite you along when I go into my property, but it's best I don't.'

'I heard nothing, Molloy.'

Then Miller's phone rang. He answered it, turning away from Molloy for a moment.

'He's what? Christ, yes, I'll go there now. You come along too, Steffi. And tell Gibb. I'm sure he'll want to be there.' He hung up.

'Problems?' Molloy said.

'You heard about that council member being found murdered this morning?'

'I did.'

'It's not him. James Merchant is alive and well.'

'How come?'

'Merchant called the police. It's somebody else entirely.'

'Who?'

'That's what I need to find out.'

THIRTY-FIVE

'We took prints off him of course,' Kate Murphy said as they all stood round looking at the man on the steel table, 'but nothing's come back yet.' She smiled as Andy Watt came in.

'I'll hunt them up,' Miller said to her.

'Glad you could join the party,' Gibb said to Watt.

'I've had other urgent business to take care of.'

Gibb rolled his eyes.

'Maybe Maggie Parks could move things along quicker,' Watt said.

'I'll give her a call, Frank, see what I can do.' He left the PM suite and Miller put his phone away.

'Death by spear?' Watt said.

Kate shook her head. 'No, believe it or not. That came post mortem. His neck was snapped. Then the spear driven through him.'

'Good God, why would anybody want to do that?'
Steffi Walker said.

'I wish I had the answer.'

As they stood around the body, Gibb came back in.
'They said they were about to send the results through
when I phoned.'

'By carrier pigeon?' Watt said.

'Well, we got the results now. Or we will have
when the text comes through.' He looked at his screen.
'His name is Thomas Williams. He was fingerprinted
for housebreaking, and he served minimal time because
it was a first offence.' Gibb kept reading. 'Get this; he
had broken into George Stone's house. Three months
ago.'

'Stone's name keeps popping up here,' Miller said.
'We should have another word with him.'

'I need to have a word with you. In private,' Gibb
said to Watt and they walked outside.

'What's up, Paddy?'

'I hate to admit this, but you were right; after our
prints were eliminated, the others Maggie found
belong to Eve Ross. The mad cow was in my flat, Andy,
and I am not happy about that.'

'Aw, Jesus. Look, I'm sorry, Paddy. I'm not going to
drag you into this. I'll go back to your place and pack
my things.'

'Of course you won't. We're not running from this

woman. I'll have another lock added. I'll give the bloke we use a call. The guy who comes out after we've booted a door in. He's a good guy.'

'You mean he'll give you a discount.'

'Don't say it like it's a bad thing.'

DS Julie Stott was sitting in the office, at a desk along from Hazel Carter.

'Why are you not at home with the kids, Hazel?' Julie said.

'My mum's got them for the day. Well, the weekend actually.'

'I could think of better things to do on my weekend. Spa, bar, nice restaurant. Did you toss a coin and lose?'

Hazel laughed. 'No fun on my own.'

'You don't have a boyfriend?'

'I've been out on a few dates, but when we've been at dinner, I tell them that I have two young kids, and then offer to pick up the tab for the meal, so they don't think I'm after a freebie. Only one took up the offer, and still didn't want a second date.'

'How about online dating?'

'To be honest, I was thinking about that. I haven't done anything about it yet though.'

'You should.'

They were looking at the videos and photos they had taken at the Robert Molloy unveiling. Then she noticed somebody in the crowd.

'Hazel, come and take a look at this. Tell me what you think.'

Hazel came over to Julie's desk and looked at the face at the point where the video was paused. 'What about him?'

'Take a look at these photos from the bank building. We had a group of onlookers at the front of the building, but only a small group at the back. He was at the back. I remember thinking what a weirdo he looked.'

'Oh yeah, there he is.'

She played with the mouse on the computer. More photos popped up.

'And here he is again. Frank told me to take photos at a scene, just in case. Even if it's with our own phones. And there he is again this morning. But there was only one difference this time.'

She showed Hazel.

'Oh my God. Give Frank a call. He needs to hear about this.'

THIRTY-SIX

'The police are coming here?' James Merchant said. He and George Stone were in the gentlemen's club in Princes Street.

'Yes, I already told you that. Why don't you try paying attention for once?'

'A detective?'

'No, Sting and his friends. Of course, a fucking detective.' He snapped his fingers and one of the waiters came across. 'Two whiskies and show the copper in to us when he arrives.'

'Right away, sir.'

'And where's Sanquer today?'

'How would I know?' The waiter walked away.

'Who stuck a broom up his arse?' Stone said.

'Never mind that, George. What are we going to say to the detective?'

'We? Don't fucking involve me in your shenanigans. I was at home with the wife watching TV.'

'Aw, have a serious word with yourself. You're not going to back me up?'

Stone laughed. 'Of course I am. You should see your face; it's redder than a baboon's arse.' He saw the waiter coming back with a drinks tray and a man and woman walking beside him.

'Talking of a baboon's arse, here's the old wank with the drinks. And look at this, he hasn't even had the decency to formally come and tell us our visitors are here. Old pish flap.'

'Here's your drinks.' The waiter put the glasses down and walked away.

'Detective Miller, we meet again. And who is this young lady you have with you?' Stone said.

'Detective Sergeant Steffi Walker.'

'Take a seat. Can I get you a drink?'

'Two sparkling waters, please,' Miller said as they sat down. The club didn't have air conditioning and Miller was sweating.

'You been hiding out here all day?' Miller asked Merchant.

'I would hardly call it hiding. I'm here with my friend and as I'm fully aware I haven't broken the law, and the victim did by stealing my wallet, I am under no illusion as to my rights.' He reached forward and picked up his drink.

Stone laughed. 'Chill the beans there, Jimmy. I'm sure the good detective here is just wanting to ask you a few questions. Like, who nicked your wallet?'

'Who nicked your wallet?' Miller said.

'I was in a bar and was leaving for the night. When I got home in the taxi, my wallet was gone, but I had some cash in my pocket so I paid the cab in cash.'

'And you reported it missing when?'

'I was going to do it last night but it was late and I was drunk.'

'You went home from the bar last night?' Steffi said.

'No, he came to my house. I asked him to come and discuss some plans with me,' Stone said.

'The council working out of hours with somebody who has a bid in for New Town North?' Steffi said. 'Bit unethical, isn't it?'

Again, Stone laughed. 'She's spunky, Miller. She's a keeper. But to answer your question, Jimmy and I go way back. We've been friends for a long time, and just because we chose similar career paths that might conflict along the way, we are nonetheless good friends and will remain so.'

'Why don't you just tell me why you were both at Preston House last night?' Miller said.

For the first time, Stone didn't seem so sure of himself. 'I don't know what you're talking about.'

'Now you're sounding like a schemie who's been caught stealing a car.'

Miller sensed a presence behind him and turned to look at the waiter standing with the tray and two glasses.

'Thank you,' Miller said, taking them.

'You are very welcome,' the man said, and put the empty tray on a stand. He moved over to another table and started tidying up a newspaper.

'Back to Preston House,' Miller said. 'Why were you there last night, George?'

'Why would you think I was there?'

'An old man was out walking his dog. He has insomnia. He saw your car. He gave me the license plate.'

Stone smirked. 'He's mistaken. That wasn't my plate he saw.'

'That's true, but it *is* registered to one of your work vans.'

There was silence around the table. Stone wasn't smirking now. 'So there was a car there with one of my work van's number on it.'

'A silver Range Rover. You drive one of those, don't you?'

'Doesn't mean anything.'

'For God's sake, don't you understand what's going on here? A young man had his neck broken and a spear shoved through him. Your architect died the same way. You're the connection here, Stone.'

'That's a stretch, detective.'

'I think you're playing with fire,' Steffi said. 'There was a symbol on the wall where Rick Dempsey was found. The only thing it looked like was the symbol for Anubis, the Egyptian God of the dead.'

'Somebody was playing games. Trying to throw you off the scent. Understandable.'

Miller shook his head. 'You don't understand. Or maybe you do. Detective Walker here did a bit of background research on you and Dempsey. She wasn't surprised to see that you had snapped up the old university buildings at Craiglockhart. But let me ask you this; you gave us a little bit of the history of the main building when we were there, but do you know the full history of the place?'

'Of course not. I just wanted that building to be a feature in the sales pitch. Why, what's wrong with the place?'

'Nothing,' Steffi said, 'but it's who owned it that's interesting.'

'It was owned by some old geezer, Montgomery Highmore.'

'That's correct. He was a businessman in the eighteen hundreds. He was also an occultist. He went under the name Gabriel Morte. Gabriel means—'

'The Angel of Death,' Merchant interrupted.

'Let her finish, Jimmy. Fucking interrupting. Go on, hen.'

'He was rich and very charismatic. He built a house on an estate. His fame and fortune grew, but unlike some other occultists in the past, he had a great following. Something like these fake churches are like today, except those religious nut jobs take your money and fill your head with broken glass.'

Miller put a hand on her arm, sensing that she was getting heated about the fake churches. He looked at her and nodded. She carried on.

'As I was saying, he built a house on a piece of land he bought. It was deemed a beautiful project. A mansion in its own grounds. Highmore House it was called. People thought it was magnificent. Until the shenanigans. The orgies, the wild drinking parties. It all got out of hand. Some of the more upstanding locals got together and demanded Highmore stop.

'He refused. A fight broke out in the house between the locals and the members of his cult, and a fire broke out. It completely destroyed the house. The locals stopped people from trying to put it out and it burnt to the ground. Montgomery Highmore died in the fire. It was cleared, the land sold, and a family bought it and built on top of the foundations of High-more House. Later on, that too caught fire and you can see the remains today. Some say the second house burnt down because it was cursed.'

'I don't believe in ghosts,' Stone said.

'That's not the point,' Miller said. 'The story of how Highmore died is widely documented, even mentioning that his followers attacked the locals with spears.'

Stone looked at him for a moment before bursting out laughing. 'This is bollocks.'

'No, it's not, George,' Merchant said. 'You've got to tell him.'

'Shut up, Jimmy.'

'No, George, you and I have known each other for a long time, as you said, so you have to trust me. He needs to know.'

'For fuck's sake.'

'I need to know what?' Miller said.

'You're right, we were there last night,' Merchant said.

'Don't leave out the bit where you had your nob out,' Stone said.

'We were there, having a look around. George wants to buy the place, build houses on the land. Have a big mansion there or maybe a hotel. So we were exploring it and there's these passageways and steps that go down to another level. I got attacked and was pulled into another corridor. I think there were steps there too, but I fought the guy after he took my wallet.'

'Did you see who it was?'

Merchant shook his head. 'It was dark, and we were struggling.'

Steffi sat up straighter. 'You realise that you just put yourself at the top of the list of suspects?'

Stone looked at him. 'I told you if you said anything, they would think you killed that twat.'

'Show them the video, then.'

'Just as well you're my good friend or I'd have skelped you a long time ago.' Stone brought his iPhone out and opened the photos to the video he'd shot the night before. Gave his phone to Miller.

'As you can see, I was sitting in my car, thinking he'd buggered off. When I put the full beams on, here he comes, doing a fair impression of Jesse Owen. He gets up to the car and... well, you can see for yourself.'

Miller watched Merchant running for his life. There was a bit of jumping about with the video as he got in the car.

Fucking drive, George! They're trying to kill me!

Stone didn't talk but got the car in reverse and swung it round, but not before it captured some faces first. The one at the front was the man they'd found dead that morning. They were wearing cloaks and clutching spears.

Miller watched as the phone was handed to Merchant, who shot the video through the back window, watching as spears were thrown at them. Then Stone turned left and booted it back the way they had come. Merchant had kept the video rolling until they were well away north of Penicuik and then he started it up again as they pulled into a petrol station, both men getting out to fill up and making sure to look up at the security cameras and again when they went into the shop to buy some crisps.

'Neither of us killed that bloke,' Stone said.

Miller handed the phone back. 'I believe you. You were well outnumbered there. But let me ask you something; did you just disturb them or were they waiting for you?'

'I have no doubt they were waiting. If they were all down there, they wouldn't have heard us. The walls are thick. They had to be expecting us.'

'How would they know when you were going?'

'I have no idea. Jimmy and I only discussed it here, and we always made sure nobody was eavesdropping.'

Miller nodded. 'I'm going there after dark to have a look around.'

'What? You're mental,' Merchant said. 'No offense.'

'None taken. But I'm going tonight.'

'I'm going with you,' Stone said.

'I can't allow that.'

'Listen, I'm going to be there one way or another. Let's just say, I'm showing you the way round there.'

'Okay. I'm sure whoever was there was scared off. We'll be there around nine o'clock. I'll pick you up at home.'

Stone took his wallet out and took out a business card. 'Meet me there instead.'

THIRTY-SEVEN

It wasn't quite dark in Jean Melrose's street but shaded as the sun was heading west, slipping down towards the horizon.

Rose, Kerry Hamilton's assistant, walked up to Jean's front door with a black, leather folder in one hand. She knocked hard, then waiting for a few minutes, put her finger on the doorbell. And kept it there until the door was answered.

'What?' Mark said after opening the door.

'I'm with the bank. I'm here to talk to Jean Melrose.'

'She's not here. I don't know where she is or how long she'll be.' He made to shut the door.

'Did she get the notices?' Rose said.

'What are you talking about?' Mark replied, irritation in his voice. He looked like he hadn't slept for a week. His hair was tousled and he had a bruise round one eye.

'She's defaulted on six mortgage payments in a row. Now the bank is repossessing the house. I'm here to give formal notice to her. I need to come in to inspect the property.'

His eyes went a little wide. 'You're not coming in here.'

'I'm with the bank. I can come in. I'll show you my credentials.' She held out a leather wallet and flipped it open. Inside was a piece of paper. *How many inside?* was written on it.

She put it away and nodded to him.

He looked at her. Stuck two fingers up at her in a derogatory way. Rolled his eyes.

Two people. Upstairs.

She nodded to him. 'If you're not letting me in, we'll be back. Next week.'

She thought he looked genuinely terrified as he shut the door. Rose walked back out to the road and crossed over and got in the car. They were out of sight of the upstairs windows at this point.

Robert Molloy and Adrian Jackson were sitting in the back of Molloy's BMW, in front of a van.

'There are two of them,' Rose said from the front.

'He could be lying,' Jackson said.

'He could be, but you didn't see his face.'

'You think he's genuine, Rose?'

'I do. If it was my decision, I'd say go.'

Molloy looked to Jackson. 'Your men are up to this?'

Jackson smiled. 'They used to do this for a living. Dealing with a couple of arseholes they could do with their eyes closed.'

Molloy nodded. 'Give them a call.'

Jackson dialled a number and when it was answered, he spoke one word: 'Go.'

The back doors of the van opened and closed without the slightest sound. Two men in black ran down the side street, one of them carrying a black holdall. There was a lower wall with a hedge atop. Further down, the wall was taller with metal poles sticking up from it. There was no fence attached anymore. The men were up and over the wall without breaking stride.

The garden was dark. They sprinted across the side garden and stopped at a small window. The bag was put down. It was already unzipped. The first man took out a suction cup, cut a hole in the glass and reached in to unlock the window.

He slid it up as the second man put the tools away. First man in, second man handed over the bag and followed.

This was a utility room off the kitchen, and they

each took out a silenced rifle and put on a gas mask. They hadn't spoken a word to each other. They had rehearsed this, and after looking at plans of the house, could go around it blindfolded. They stepped out into the kitchen. Clear. Same with the living room.

They heard voices upstairs and climbed them, putting weight at the edge of the runners, stepping up carefully, pointing their rifles.

'I don't fucking care!' they heard a man's voice shout.

They stepped onto the landing. Checked each room. Nothing. Then more shouting coming along from a corridor that led straight ahead.

'If you don't tell us where that fucking money is, I'm going to give you an overdose like we did to that other bitch!'

They walked along silently. This led into the other wing of the house.

There was a door open. A man was standing in front of a young woman who was tied to a chair. There was a lamp on in the room. Both men clearly saw a man and woman standing in front of the victim.

'Fuck it. She doesn't know anything. Let's just kill the bitch,' the female said.

'She's already fucking dead, you stupid cow! You gave her too much. Now we'll have to kill the others so there's no witnesses.'

The first soldier took out a flash bang and threw it into the room as the female stepped forward with the needle.

There were screams as the soldiers entered the room. They took a look at the subjects and knew they wouldn't need guns.

The man had a knife. The first soldier stepped forward and disarmed him in text book style.

As the noise subsided, and the smoke dissipated, the female was crouching, coughing, and had her hands over her ears. Then she saw the man in black and screeched like a wounded animal as she saw her boyfriend being restrained.

'Get your fucking hands off him!' she said, taking a run at the first man, but number two stepped in front of her. 'You think you can stop me? Hard man going to hit a girl?'

And that's exactly what he had been trained to do. He wasn't hitting a woman, he was hitting a target. He punched her and she fell sideways, then he was on top of her and before she knew what was happening, he'd put cable ties on her wrists behind her back.

He stood up and put the tip of the silenced rifle on her cheek next to her eye. 'Move and I will fucking kill you. Understand?' She said nothing. He kicked her in the ribcage just below the armpit, a place that had no muscle covering it; a kick designed to cause pain. It worked. She nodded after yelling out.

Number one had the man sitting up while number two went over to the female in the chair. Abi Melrose. Very dead.

'Where's the other girl?' One said to the man.

'I'm telling you nothing.'

'Really now?'

'Yeah, and you coppers can do fuck all about it. I want a lawyer.'

'Here's a surprise for you then, sonny; we're not coppers.' He reached over and grabbed the man's little finger on his right hand and bent it back. They could hear the snap. As he started to scream, a gloved hand was put over his mouth.

'I'm going to take the glove off and you'll tell me, or the next thing that gets broken is your manhood.' One grabbed the man's crotch. 'Where is she?'

'Down a bit in another room. With her boyfriend.'

He squeezed the man's scrotum tighter. 'Are we going to find any surprises in there? Anybody else with a knife and a gun.'

The man shook his head.

'If we do, we'll kill you and her. As it is, you're getting a free pass, but if there's anybody else there, I'll shoot you in the gut and let your blood mix with stomach acid until you die a slow death.'

'There's nobody else there, I promise.'

Number Two left and came back a couple of minutes later. 'They're alive and well.'

'Good. Make the call. Tell them to stay put. They're safe.'

Number Two left and One let go of the guy's scrotum. 'Pity. I was enjoying myself there, at the thought of cutting your dick off.' He stood up and kicked the man hard in the guts, winding him.

Molloy took the call. He and Jackson were still in the back of the car. 'Your men are good,' he said. 'I'm impressed.'

'Praise indeed.'

Molloy got out of the car and crossed the road to the little Honda sitting on the other side. The driver wound her window down.

'Chief Superintendent Bridge, your daughter is alive and will be coming out shortly. One of my men has made a call saying they heard gunshots coming from the house. Completely false of course, no shots were fired. But that will bring the cavalry. The two people you are looking for have been tied up, brought downstairs and have been incapacitated. My men are bringing your daughter out now. You can go and see her.'

'I don't know what to say.'

'You don't have to say anything, and nothing is expected in return. Somebody hurt a friend of mine, so I had to gain entry. Into my own house, I may add. I own the property, therefore, no warrants were needed. I simply had two friends check the place out, they were attacked and had to subdue their attackers. But they're shy, so they left. End of story.'

Jeni Bridge started crying. 'My little girl is safe?'

'A little bruised and frightened, but luckily one of my men is a trained medic. He checked her over. She's scared. She wants her mum. Her friend is being escorted back to Glasgow. With a warning that he shouldn't see your daughter again, or the men who attacked Lynn will be told Mark tipped us off.'

'Mr Molloy, I don't know how to thank you.'

'I already said, no thanks needed. Just throw the book at the bastards.'

'Count on it.'

They watched as the van pulled out from behind them and drove up to the gates in front of the driveway. They opened and the two men in black came out with a young man and woman. Lynn Bridge ran over to her mother who met her halfway.

'I hear sirens. Time I wasn't here,' Molloy said, and got back into the car. The two men in black got into the van. The BMW pulled in behind it and the two vehicles were gone.

'I'm sorry, Mum,' Lynn said. 'I didn't mean to treat you so badly.'

Jeni looked over at the house 'Don't worry about it,' she said as the first armed response unit pulled in. 'Sit in my car. I have to talk to these men.'

Angel stood quietly weeping in the corner, her arms wrapped around herself. *'Why, Eve, why?'* she said, her voice sounding strained.

Eve lay on the bed, her eyes open, staring into nothing.

'We could have been so strong together. We could have gone on to better things. Done anything we wanted to. Just like all the things we talked about.'

But Eve wasn't listening.

Eve was gone.

THIRTY-EIGHT

'You know what a ha-ha is?' George Stone asked as they walked across the field.

'Yes, I know what a ha-ha is,' Miller said, as they approached the wall and climbed out.

'Well then. Not everybody does. Bloody show off.'

'Just keep focused on the job at hand.'

'Listen, if you and the missus fancy one of those townhouses I'm building up at Craiglockhart, I'm doing similar ones down overlooking Newhaven harbour. I could get you a good deal.'

'No thanks. We like where we live.'

'Suit yourself. The offer's always there if you change your mind.'

'Just show me where this doorway is.'

'It's down there,' Stone said, pointing to the doorway that was hidden from the outside world.

Miller thought Stone must have been mistaken at first because it just looked like a recess. But when they went down, he took out his flashlight and shone it around and saw the opening.

They went in and along the corridor to the dead end, and Stone pushed against the wall and it opened. He took Miller along the passageways until they came to the stairs, his own light leading the way.

They went down to the hexagonal room with the other corridors leading off.

'Which was the one that Merchant went down?' Miller asked.

'That one there,' Stone said, pointing with his torch. 'I mean, I didn't hear anything so I'm just going by what Jimmy told me. Then a part of the wall opened.' Miller went along and pushed on the walls but nothing happened.

'I don't see anything,' Miller said. 'Stone? Did you hear what I said?' No reply.

Miller thought for a second he had been duped until he went back into the hexagonal room and saw the men with spears standing either side of Stone, one of them holding a spear to his throat. They were wearing full attire now, not like they had been in the film made on Stone's phone. The robes they wore were white and gold, and they wore face masks with eye holes cut in them.

A third man, dressed the same way but who was obviously much more powerful than the others, turned to look at Miller.

'You just couldn't leave it alone, could you?' he said, his voice slightly muffled.

'Leave what alone? Your little pervy gathering downstairs?'

The man laughed. 'You would not understand in a million years.'

'You mean about Montgomery Highmore? I think I know everything there is to know about this place.'

'You haven't even scratched the surface. He was a man with a vision, a man well before his time. He had the whole world in his hands.'

'One thing he didn't have that we have today; the internet. There's everything on there about everything. Videos on how to make a pie, or fix your lawnmower. How to shift gears on a big American truck, if that's what you're into. There is also an interesting video about this place. Put up by a local photographer. There are also many articles about Preston House and how it was built on the foundation of Highmore House. Very interesting.'

'Again, you've merely scratched the surface.'

'Despite your disguise, we know who you are, Colonel.'

Colonel Sanquer took his headgear off. 'I must

admit to being surprised. We guard our privacy with the utmost vigour.'

'It came to me after I asked myself, how come Stone there only talks to his friend in the sanctity of that club, yet somebody knew he was going to be sneaking about here last night? It had to be somebody in the club, but who?'

'Very clever.'

'Mr Stone there said you were always hovering about. Like the other one today. Again, we figured it out with the help of modern technology. You see, two of my team were going through video footage they'd shot on their phones and they saw you, at Robert Molloy's unveiling of the New Town North project. They looked at the other crime scene photos, and there you were again, with the other waiter from the club.'

'That means nothing.'

'Stuffing the pages down Rick Dempsey's throat was a clue; pages from *A Dance with the Devil* by Gabriel Morte, who we all know and love as Montgomery Highmore.'

Colonel Sanquer laughed again. 'Okay, you've got me; this house was Montgomery's and not to be pulled down and built on. It's sacrilege. This place was fine on its own, just ticking away nicely. We don't need the George Stones of this world coming along and tearing it apart.'

'What about the man we found on the scaffolding this morning?'

'He failed. He made a sacrifice. We don't tolerate failure.'

'I think you failed too, didn't you?'

'Quite the opposite, I would think. You're here, and you're going to be taken down to the sacrifice chamber where you will be slaughtered. But since there doesn't need to be a warning sent to anybody this time, we'll just get rid of your remains after we kill you.'

'Are you getting this?' Miller said out loud. Nothing in reply. 'For God's sake, now would be a good time.'

'A good time to kill you both, I agree.' He turned to look at the two men. George Stone's face was a picture in the flickering light of the oil torches. 'Kill them now.'

'Armed police! Drop that fucking spear, now!' The armed police officer shouted as he came barrelling down the steps. Followed by Lloyd Masters, commander of the tactical unit. He pointed his Heckler and Koch at Sanquer.

'He used to be in the army too,' Miller said to the colonel. 'And he knows how to use guns.'

More armed officers stormed in as the two men dressed in robes let George Stone go. One of them was the waiter from the club that afternoon.

'You bastard,' Stone said to him. 'Listening to my conversations.'

'You were an easy man to listen to. You have a big mouth.'

Stone said nothing more as the men were taken away, but Sanquer stopped to look at him. 'This place is cursed by the ghost of Gabriel Morte. You might want to take that on board.' Then he was led away.

'Good plan of yours, Miller. But was it true about the photos? That Sanquer was at the crime scenes?'

'Yes, that was true.'

They walked out of the underground chamber and into fresh air again.

'You know what, Miller? This place is a crap hole. I've changed my mind about building here.'

'Nothing to do with the curse?' Miller said. Stone ignored him.

THIRTY-NINE

Maggie Parks hit the button on the remote key fob sounding the car horn, despite it being late and the likelihood of disturbing the neighbours. Too bad, she thought. The drunks don't keep it down when they're walking home at three o'clock on a Sunday morning, singing and puking.

She walked over from the small car park in front of the church and a woman bumped into her.

'So sorry,' she said, and carried on over to her car.

Maggie took her mobile phone out. 'Oh, hi. No, that's fine. Stay out as late as you want. I'm tired so I'll be in bed when you get home. Bye, Andy. Love you too.'

She walked down the steps to the front door. There were no lights on in the house. She unlocked the door and went in, switching on a light. Then she put the living room lights on. Then she went through to the kitchen where a bottle of wine was waiting for her.

Then the faintest sound of the front door opening.

Angel walked along the hallway. It was more exciting when she was with Eve, but now Eve wouldn't hold her back. She'd just kill this bitch and leave. Go back to where she used to be.

She was undecided how she should kill Andy's new mistress. Knife? Strangulation with a ligature? It would be easy to roll a towel and put it round her neck. Blunt force trauma? Maybe make it look like a hanging like she'd done with Simon down in Dumfries.

The thought excited her. She was buzzing as she stepped into the kitchen ready to overpower the bitch. She looked around in confusion when she got in.

'Hello, Eve,' Andy Watt said.

Angel looked over at the kitchen door which was ajar. There was no sign of Maggie. She stepped closer to Watt, who was casually leaning against the kitchen counter. She took a step forward towards him. He didn't budge.

'I'm not Eve. I'm Angel. Eve died earlier tonight.'

'Sit down. Let's talk,' Watt said, not moving.

'You don't care that Eve died?'

'I know she didn't die, Angel. I know she's still in there, inside your head. You became dominant, I understand that, but don't you think Eve should be on her meds?'

Angel laughed. 'It's too late for that. Simon's dead. He's the one who gave Eve her meds. He was holding us back. He needed to go. I helped him depart this world. Eve was upset but I told her it was for the best.'

'Take a seat. I want to speak to Eve.'

'I told you Eve's dead, or weren't you listening?'

'She doesn't have to be though, does she? You could bring her back.'

'With the meds. I don't have any, and I was sick of her being so nice to you. I don't think you deserved it and I told her so.' Angel walked towards the butcher's knife that was sitting on the counter and looked across the kitchen table at Andy.

'I'd like to say I'm sorry for killing you, Andy, but I'm not.' She lifted the knife higher and walked to the side of the table before her whole brain exploded and her body danced uncontrollably before she fell and hit the kitchen floor.

'Jesus, that was a bit close for comfort,' Watt said to Frank Miller, who was still holding the Taser. He let go of the trigger but the wires were still attached. Percy Purcell came in behind him with two uniforms.

'We had to get it recorded.'

Watt knelt down beside the woman who was lying motionless on the floor. He saw a flicker in her eyes.

'Andy, you came to me. I knew you would. Please take me away from Angel. She's mean and makes me do things. I love you, Andy.'

'We'll get you help, Eve.'

Then the eyes changed. 'Get your fucking hands off me,' Angel said.

The uniforms held her down and handcuffed her after Miller took the prongs out. Angel started struggling.

The force doctor, a new man to the team, came in, opened his medical bag, and took out a syringe and injected her in the arm.

'This will sedate her without compromising her. She needs to be taken to the Royal Scottish right away.'

After Angel stopped struggling, she was still awake, but all the fight had gone out of her.

'I love you, Andy,' Eve said.

Paramedics came in and got her into a chair and strapped her in.

Gibb and Maggie came in from the back garden as the others filed out.

'Listen, I can go and stay with one of my daughters. She's pregnant and the spare room will be for the bairn, but I can kip on her floor until the bairn arrives.'

'Shut up, Andy,' Maggie said, stepping forward and putting her arms around him. 'I'm just glad you're safe.' She looked at Gibb. 'I'm sure Andy can stay as long as he needs to?'

Gibb nodded. 'Of course he can. But the minute he starts sleepwalking...'

'Thanks. And thanks to you all for helping me with Eve,' he said when Maggie let him go.

'Poor woman needs help,' Purcell said. 'I've only ever seen one person with multiple personality disorder before, and it's hellish.'

'The more she let the meds get out of her system, the more she became Angel,' Miller said.

'Maybe one day we'll find out what caused this disorder,' Gibb said. 'She was a nice person when we met her in Langholm. A very good doctor.'

'We'll do an investigation,' Purcell said, 'and that will mean you talking to Standards, Watt.'

'I'll tell them everything I know.' *Except maybe admitting I slept with her.*

'It can wait though. I'll make sure she gets to the psychiatric hospital.' Purcell left.

'Despite me messing up, you lot were still standing behind me. I appreciate it.'

'Aw, listen to this, Watt getting all soppy,' Gibb said.

'Don't listen to him, Andy. You know we're all behind you,' Maggie said.

'Now Purcell knows about you and Paddy,' Watt said.

'I spoke to him on the way over,' Miller said. 'He saw nothing. He didn't see Maggie come down the steps. And Maggie was outside until he left.'

'He's not daft though.'

'Just leave it at that, Andy,' Maggie said.

FORTY

Monday morning brought rain with it.

'That's better,' Robert Molloy said, looking out of his office window onto Waverley station. 'I thought Auld Reekie was going soft in her old age.' He turned to face the room.

Kerry Hamilton and Adrian Jackson were sitting. There was a knock at the door and Greg Sampson showed Molloy's guest in.

'George, come in. We've been waiting for you.'

George Stone was followed into the room by Michael Molloy. Robert shook his hand. 'Come, sit down. Drink? Coffee?'

'I'm fine thanks, Robert.' He looked at the others. 'Kerry. Adrian.'

They nodded to him.

'Right, without further ado, let's get down to business. We thought about your proposal for us to join forces, and we have decided that we think it's in everybody's best interests that we work as a consortium. I know that your reputation is fucked after your name appeared in the papers over the weekend.'

'I don't know who leaked my name to the press,' Stone complained.

'It was inevitable, considering how many people were involved. However, let's focus on the future; as of right now, one of my representatives is speaking with the family who own the estate, and they have been made an offer they can't refuse. I have trucks on the site right now, pumping concrete right down to where those deviants played with their spears, after I had structural engineers out there yesterday.

'Preston House will be renamed, and the house will be rebuilt to its former glory and made into a hotel. On the field where the ha-ha is, we are going to build a glass dome, where we can cater for outside weddings without the risk of marquees being blown away. I have an architect drawing those plans up now.'

'Sounds good to me,' Stone said.

'Now you're under our umbrella,' Kerry said, 'all projects are being put in the pot, including yours at Merchiston. And we're all sharing the profits.'

'With the four of us in business together,' Jackson

continued, 'we can easily fend off bids from upstarts. Cut them off at the knees before they become too big.'

'Agreed.'

'We get new offices,' Michael said, 'where all the staff will be amalgamated and restructured. If any staff member isn't happy, they can walk.'

Stone nodded. 'What about Jimmy Merchant?'

'We need him in the council, so he stays,' Robert said.

Stone nodded again. 'Better the devil you know,' he said.

AFTERWORD

First of all, I would like to reiterate that this is a work of fiction. My characters are fictitious and the story is made up. The New Town North Project is real, as is the building where Rick Dempsey is found. That's it for real life. Every else is fiction. I would also like to add that the opinions of the characters are not mine.

I would like to thank Julie Dumbarton, an artist in Langholm, Scotland, for letting me use her gallery in my book. Check her out on Facebook. She has some fantastic work.

And thanks to the usual gang – in no particular order – Louise Unsworth Murphy, Wendy Haines, Julie Stott, Fiona and Adrian Jackson, Jeni Bridge, Michelle Barragan, Tracey Devonshire, Evelyn Bell, Merrill Astill Blount, Vanessa Kerrs, Bejay Roles and last but not least, Barbara Bartley. Thank you all for your support. You are all fantastic!

Thank you also to my wife, who keeps the dogs entertained while I work; my daughters, Stephanie and Samantha.

And thank you to you, the reader, for tagging along on this journey with me. You make it all worthwhile. And if I could ask you to please leave a review, that would really help me.

'Til next time!

John Carson
New York
December 2018

ABOUT THE AUTHOR

John Carson is originally from Edinburgh, Scotland, but now lives with his wife and family in New York State. And two dogs. And four cats.

www.johncarsonauthor.com

Printed in Great Britain
by Amazon